COLTONS

Meet the Coltons—a California dynasty with a legacy of privilege and power.

HOLLY LAMB: *Overnight Cinderella.* She's been in love with her gorgeous, serious-minded boss since the first day she started work, but Blake has never treated her with anything more than friendly respect. Until he invites her to a dance, and this virgin transforms herself into a sexy siren…

BLAKE FALLON: *A hero for Holly.* His undemanding assistant has loyally stood by his side throughout countless crises, but can he prove his mettle—and love—when Holly most needs his support?

JOE COLTON: *Town patriarch.* Though he and his long-lost wife have opened their home to the townspeople during this crisis, this selfless man has more planned for the community that saw him through his long ordeal!

THE COLTONS

A HASTY WEDDING

CARA COLTER

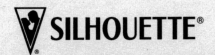

First published in Great Britain 2003
Silhouette Books, Eton House, 18-24 Paradise Road,
Richmond, Surrey TW9 1SR

© Harlequin Books S.A. 2001

Special thanks and acknowledgement are given to Cara Colter
for her contribution to THE COLTONS series.

ISBN 0 373 38719 9

139-0503

Printed and bound in Spain
by Litografía Rosés S.A., Barcelona

CARA COLTER

Readers often tell author Cara Colter the only thing they don't like about her books is that they end too soon! Cara was delighted to be asked to write for THE COLTONS series, especially since the longer format allowed her the opportunity to satisfy reader requests *and* develop her characters more deeply. Holly and Blake, the hero and heroine of *A Hasty Wedding*, are a dynamic couple who have transformed the early challenges of their lives into their greatest strengths. This is a theme that is profoundly and personally meaningful to Cara.

Cara lives in a remote area of British Columbia, and so the experience of working with other writers on THE COLTONS series was a delightful one for her. 'I am absolutely in awe of the imagination, talent and intelligence of the women who wrote the series.'

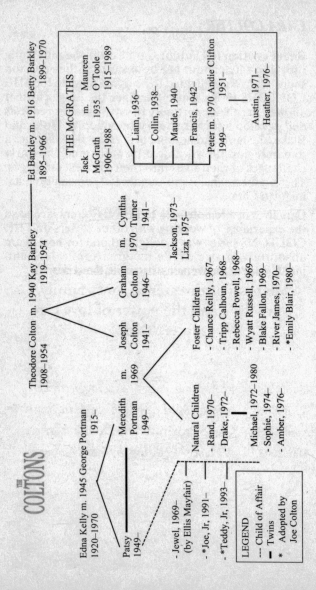

THE COLTONS

Edna Kelly m. 1945 George Portman
1920–1970   1915–

Theodore Colton m. 1940 Kay Barkley
1908–1954   1919–1954

Ed Barkley m. 1916 Betty Barkley
1895–1966   1899–1970

THE McGRATHS

Jack McGrath   m. 1935   Maureen O'Toole
1906–1988   1915–1989

- Liam, 1936–
- Collin, 1938–
- Maude, 1940–
- Francis, 1942–
- Peter m. 1970 Andie Clifton
  1949–   1951–
  - Austin, 1971–
  - Heather, 1976–

Patsy
1949–

Meredith Portman
1949–

m. 1969

Joseph Colton
1941–

Graham Colton
1946–

m. 1970   Cynthia Turner
1941–

- Jackson, 1973–
- Liza, 1975–

Foster Children
- Chance Reilly, 1967–
- Tripp Calhoun, 1968–
- Rebecca Powell, 1968–
- Wyatt Russell, 1969–
- Blake Fallon, 1969–
- River James, 1970–
- *Emily Blair, 1980–

Natural Children
- Rand, 1970–
- Drake, 1972–

Michael, 1972–1980
- Sophie, 1974–
- Amber, 1976–

- Jewel, 1969–
  (by Ellis Mayfair)
- *Joe, Jr, 1991–
- *Teddy, Jr, 1993–

LEGEND
- - - Child of Affair
▬ Twins
* Adopted by Joe Colton

Don't worry

THE COLTONS

haven't finished yet!

The Coltons
**When California's most talked about
dynasty is threatened, only family,
privilege and the power of love can
protect them!**

**To Jeff Shatzko
the son of my heart**

One

The knife was sharp and cold, the tip of it pressed into the delicate flesh where her neck and her jawbone met.

Her afternoon had slipped from mundane to perilous in a single tick of the second hand on the old grandfather clock that sat in the corner of her office, and Holly Lamb waited for her life to flash before her eyes.

When it did not, she was amazed when her mind told her, with wry good humor that was totally inappropriate given the knife and the wild eyes of the young man who wielded it, that her life had really not been interesting enough first time around to take a repeat on it.

Ordinary if not particularly happy childhood, college, secretarial career. No wild passions or great loves, no untamed moments of youthful hijinks, no great accomplishments in the arts or sciences.

But even in light of that rather unexciting twenty-seven years, Holly could not persuade any regrets to come to mind. She did not suddenly wish she had accepted the invitation to bungee jump—naked—off the Prosperino Bridge. She had no regrets about not seeing the Sistine Chapel or climbing Mount Kilimanjaro.

Of course, she might have liked to know about sex.

Not "know" in a technical sense, as if movies and television hadn't educated everyone quite enough in that area. Maybe *know* wasn't quite the right word. *Experience* would be a better choice of words. While one part of her brain tried desperately to tell her that this was really not the time to be following this particular flow of thoughts, the other part continued blithely down the path, speculating what it would be like to feel so close to another human being, to have a man's lips claim your lips, and his hands touch your body with tenderness and mastery...

It came to her then, where this path was leading.

What came to her in that moment with the blade pressed sharply, in uncomfortably close proximity to her jugular, was a startling clarity of thought.

What came to her was a stunning secret that she had kept from herself for eight months. A secret that filled her with a stunning sense of warmth, again, totally inappropriate to the situation she was in.

But she held the thought, and in it she found a great well of courage and calm inside of herself. She dipped into it.

"Why don't you put the knife down?" she suggested, amazed at what was in her voice. Not just calm. But a compassion born of her new self-knowledge.

"You tell me where my sister is." Her attacker's voice was harsh, and his face was so close to hers she could feel the heat of his breath, smell his desperation.

"I don't even know *who* your sister is," she said evenly. She looked into his eyes. He was just a child, despite a faint stubble that darkened his cheeks. He might have been sixteen. His eyes were dark and wild. With fear.

Under different circumstances she might have thought he was a good-looking boy. She made herself look at him analytically. If she lived, she would have to tell the police.

His hair was dark and curly, his eyes a dark, velvety brown that reminded her of a deer caught in headlights. He was taller than her, but lithe, and wiry. His jeans and jacket were torn and dirty.

"You people," he said furiously, "think because I've made a few mistakes, I don't care about my sister? Don't you understand nothin'?"

Her clarity was holding, because she felt from her moment of studying him, she understood everything, and realized it did not have a thing to do with filling out a police report. Her voice came out gentle, filled with the most amazing tenderness.

"I understand love."

The statement amazed her, because she spoke it with such conviction.

And really, if there was a topic she had no understanding of, it was probably that one. The Lamb family were not the ones who had put the "fun" in the word *dysfunctional*. Her mother and father had divorced when she was a child, and she had harbored the secret belief it was probably her fault.

While others had tested the waters of passion and romance in college, Holly had studied.

And yet the words "I understand love" had come from some place so deep within her, she recognized it as her own soul, and she felt some subtle change in the boy, as the words, powerful in their authenticity, touched him.

The pressure of the blade on her neck faltered, eased, and then was gone. She had not even realized she had been holding her breath until she began to breathe again. She touched her neck and looked at her hand. No blood.

A deep awareness permeated her. Those words—"I understand love"—had saved her life.

The fight was gone from the boy. His thin shoulders sagged under the worn fabric of his denim jacket, and the fury of his expression melted into sad bewilderment.

"I'm so tired," he whispered. "I'm so damned tired."

"I know," she said. It was true. She could see the gray lines of fatigue around his eyes and his mouth, in the sag of his young body.

"I've been trying to find her for three weeks. Me and her, we're all we got, you know?"

She nodded, reached out tentatively and touched his arm. He stiffened, but didn't pull away.

"I went to the foster home she was in before I got put in juvvie. She wasn't there anymore. Nobody will tell me where she is. She's just little and I promised her, I promised her I'd find her as soon as I could.''

Holly listened to his voice and watched his face. Suddenly, she recognized something in the wide, lovely set of his eyes. And his words sounded so familiar. She cast back in her mind, trying to get to a place before the children had been evacuated from the Hopechest Ranch.

''She's got to have something to believe in,'' he said, broken. ''She's got to be able to believe in me.''

It came to her. A little girl looking up at her, her eyes wide, her thumb pulled out of her mouth for only a moment. *Has my brother come yet? He promised.* Then furious sucking on that thumb, as if that pushed back the tears that she wanted to cry.

''Lucille,'' Holly whispered.

The boy's head flew up, and he looked at her with tortured eyes, eyes that were afraid to believe.

''You're Tomas,'' she said with soft realization. ''You're Lucille's big brother.''

He looked back down swiftly, but not swiftly enough to hide the sudden moisture in his eyes, the twitch around his lips.

''She talks about you all the time,'' Holly said gently. ''She told me you were coming. I've been waiting for you.''

His mouth fell open, as if no one in the world, besides his little sister, had ever waited for him before.

Holly's mind clicked over the file. Mother drug-addicted. Father dead. No one *had* ever waited for him before.

''I didn't know how to find you,'' she apologized

softly. "Sometimes the records get mixed up. Especially the last couple months." She didn't want to think about the last couple months right now. "But Lucille told me not to worry. That you would come."

He came to her like he was walking out of a dream, like a wounded warrior, his head hanging, his shoulders slumping, a great and pressing weariness in him. And ever so slowly he laid his cheek on her shoulder.

It was when she gathered him to her, like the hurt child he really was, when she put one arm around his waist and stroked the beautiful dark silk of his curls with the other, that he began to cry.

The knife clattered to the floor, and when she heard the door open behind Tomas, she nudged the fallen weapon gently under the corner of her desk with her toe.

Over the heaving jean-clad shoulder, she met the eyes of her boss, Blake Fallon, director of the Hopechest Ranch, where she had come to work eight months ago as his secretary.

Gray eyes, somber, deep, quiet. His eyes reminded her of a mountain lake reflecting storm clouds and rugged, soaring peaks. The strength and wisdom of those ancient peaks seemed to be at the heart of those astonishing eyes. Even the fabulous abundance of thick sooty lashes that framed those eyes, did not detract from the impression of strength.

It was an impression that repeated itself in his features over and over again. Rugged strength proclaimed itself in the slight bump of a once-straight nose, in the uncompromising line of his mouth, in the proud angles of his chin and his cheekbones.

The theme of strength continued in the hard line of

an athletic build. Just over six feet tall, Blake Fallon was immensely broad across his shoulders, his stomach was hard and flat, his hips slim. His legs were long and tapered, the pressed jeans he was wearing clinging to the large muscle of his thigh.

Today, he was dressed casually, as he usually did when he would be spending the day in the Hopechest Ranch office. His blue plaid shirt open at the collar, tucked neatly into belted jeans, sneakers on his feet. His brown hair was short and neat, the kind of cut that policemen and Secret Service men and those who exercised authority on a regular basis seemed to gravitate to naturally.

Despite the casual dress, she knew after eight months as his secretary, there was not much casual about Blake Fallon. He had a mind as intimidating and as powerful as a steel trap. He ran the Hopechest Ranch with a seeming ease that didn't come from graduating with his MBA at the top of his class.

Her best friend, Jennifer, had given her the lowdown on Blake Fallon. He could have done anything. When he'd finished college the Fortune 500 companies had been knocking down his door. Flying him to interviews. Wining and dining him.

He'd turned his back on all that, for this.

To run a ranch for kids in trouble.

She saw him appraising the atmosphere in the room now, alert to the tension and emotion, ready, like a big jungle cat, to spring in whatever direction was needed.

''Hi, Holly. What's going on?'' His voice betrayed none of that alertness. It was deep and pleasant, relaxed. The kind of voice a cowboy used to tame a

wild horse, the kind of voice that encouraged frightened things to trust, and lonely things to believe—

She stopped her mind from going there, much too
close to the place of the secret that beat with delicate
new life in her breast.

Besides, at the sound of Blake's voice the boy
reared back from her and pivoted on his heel. His eyes
skittered around desperately for the knife, even as he
wiped his face with the sleeve of his jacket.

"This is Lucille Watkins's brother, Tomas," she
said smoothly. "Remember Lucille told us if we
couldn't find him, he'd find us?"

Blake smiled, but she saw he was gauging the boy,
and that his muscles were coiled tight, ready to deal
with all the anger and fear rolling off the boy.

"She said it about a hundred times a day," Blake
agreed, meeting the boy's defiant gaze steadily. "Tomas, I'm Blake Fallon, director of the Hopechest
Ranch."

"I don't care if you're the director of Sing-Sing.
Where's my sister? I found out she was here, but this
place is like a ghost town. All these empty buildings.
It's creepy."

"We've had an incident here," Blake said, and cast
Holly a look.

It amazed her how often they did this. Communi-
cated over kids' heads with just a look. And how
accurate they had become at reading each other.

His look asked what she had told the boy. Her look
answered *nothing. Handle with care. He's fragile.*

"What kind of incident?" Tomas asked, panicky.

"Lucille is fine. Our water was contaminated."

The boy's face went a deathly shade of pale. "Is she sick? Is she okay? If you're lying to me—"

"I have no reason to lie to you." The tone of Blake's voice never altered from that calm, steady voice that Holly had come to hear in her dreams. "She was in the hospital for a few days back a couple of months ago. As you can see, we've moved the kids off the ranch. Though the water seems free of contamination now, we're a little reluctant to bring them back just yet."

Holly knew he didn't want to tell the boy, who was upset enough already, the ugly truth. The ranch's water had been poisoned—on purpose—by a toxic substance, DMBE.

Blake had been out this morning meeting with two old friends who were working on the investigation, Rafe James, a private investigator, and Rory Sinclair, a forensic scientist from the FBI. Rory wasn't officially on the case anymore, but since he was now living in Prosperino and working out of the San Francisco FBI lab, he was keeping tabs on the case, and helping out when he could. Sergeant Kade Lummus of the Prosperino Police Department had also been at the meeting. Blake suspected they were narrowing in on a suspect, and had been doing so for some weeks.

Holly desperately wanted to know if there were any new developments. Ever since it had been discovered the water was contaminated with a substance that did not occur naturally, she was haunted by the horrid truth that someone had deliberately hurt these children—who had so rapidly become *her* children. It even worked its way into her dreams.

Terrible dreams, where a thing, a monster, poured

a substance into the wellhead. The monster kept shifting shapes in her dreams, and so did the substance.

Then she would hear Blake's voice calling her, soothing her, and she would wake, trembling, the sweat beading on her body, knowing the monster was real.

There was a monster in their midst. Someone who would poison the children she had come to love so much. Children who dropped by her office with trust held out to her in the palms of their fragile hands.

They came with small excuses. Could she mail this letter? Could she find that phone number? Could she check where a brother or sister was? But they stayed because she kept a jar of butterscotch hard candies on her desk, and a warm inviting fire going in the fireplace, and a stack of Archie comic books on the coffee table in front of the worn blue sofa.

They stayed because she never, ever pressured them to talk, but when they did, she always stopped whatever she was doing, joined them on the sofa and took the time to listen.

That was not in her job description, and neither was dispensing hugs to those who could handle them. And smiles to those who were not there yet.

Maybe it was the time with these children that had made that phrase come so confidently to her lips.

I understand love.

Her bond with them filled her in ways her life had not been filled before, and so she was eager to know what new developments Blake had managed to unearth in the ongoing investigation about the poisoning of their water system. She needed to know.

But if there was one thing her eight months on the

job here had taught her, it was that the kids came first here.

Kids who had come last everywhere else came first here.

Blake had taught her that. And he had done it without saying a single word to her. He had done it by hanging up the phone on a powerful corporate sponsor when a tough-looking towheaded boy had burst into the office moaning over a scratch on his arm. He had done it by clearing his schedule of appointments to go shoot some one-on-one hoops with a boy who was getting ready for a court date or a girl who was getting ready to go home.

He had done it by accepting the badly knitted toque one of the hugely pregnant girls at Emily's House had made for him, and wearing it with such pride. He had done it by laughing when the baseball broke the window of the dining hall. He had done it by going into the dorms at The Shack and the Homestead every single night without fail, to help tuck in, find teddy bears and read stories to the little kids and tell scary ones to the bigger kids.

He had taught her, with the expression in his eyes when he looked at these children, *his* children, that they came first.

And, somehow, before she knew it, they felt like her children, too.

But that thought—that they shared children—followed a little too swiftly on the heels of the secret that now lived inside of her, rising and falling with her every breath.

"Why don't you run Tomas over to the Coltons?" she suggested softly.

"Is that where Lucy is?" Tomas asked, frantic.

Holly smiled reassuringly at him. "The children were evacuated there when we had the water crisis. We haven't been able to bring them back yet. Lucille is going to be so excited to see you."

She looked up from the boy, to see Blake's somber gray eyes resting on her.

"Is everything okay?" he said, looking at her, one brow up and one down, the way it was when he was looking at a kid who was trying to get one past him. A lie about school. A joint in the backpack.

"Of course," she said, flashing him a quick smile.

He didn't look fooled, any more than he would have by one of the kids. "Are you sure? You look…strange."

Tomas shot her a quick, apologetic look and waited for her to tell on him, his shoulders hunched as if waiting for a blow.

"Strange?" she said lightly. "Blake Fallon, you sure know how to make a girl's day."

"I didn't know you were a girl," he teased, and gestured for Tomas to come with him. As the boy passed, he clapped a hand lightly on his shoulder. The door whispered shut behind them, and Holly went behind her desk and collapsed into her chair.

It seemed to her the secret that had come to her like a flash of blinding light when that knife had been pressed to her throat was now shining in her eyes, trembling on her lips, waiting for the whole world to see it.

Waiting for Blake Fallon to see it.

Who, in all honesty, *really* probably hadn't even noticed she was a girl.

To him, she was just part of the furniture. An efficient and indispensable secretary. Someone he liked and respected. But thought of in that way?

The you-girl-me-boy way?

She laughed shakily, tried to get her focus back on something safe. Letters that needed to be typed. Transfer documents for a couple of kids. The funding proposal that still had to go out…

It wasn't working.

Impatient with herself, she got up and tended the fire. She caught a glimpse of her reflection in the oval mirror that hung inside an ornate gilt frame on one side of the fireplace.

No wonder he hadn't noticed she was a girl.

She looked every inch the old spinster secretary who had made herself indispensable, but was about as alluring as that stout old grandfather clock in the corner. Not that she was stout. She knew she had a lovely figure—that she had gone to great and very professional lengths not to draw attention to.

Today she was wearing a below-the-knee navy skirt and matching jacket, a white silk blouse done up primly to the very place on her throat where the knife had rested only moments ago. Her pumps were sensible and added no height to her five-foot-seven frame. Her hair was light brown, virginally untouched by dyes or highlights, and kept in a no-nonsense bun. Her glasses, which she did not really need, covered her face, brow to cheekbone, and did nothing at all to show off the delicate shades of eyes so truly hazel that they appeared blue when she wore blue, brown when she wore brown, and green when she wore green.

The portrait she presented was the one she had worked to present: the world's most efficient secretary.

Growing up in the shadow of her socialite mother, who had made glamour her goddess, Holly had rejected using appearances to gain power. She wanted to be respected for what she was, not for how she looked.

What she was was hardworking, honest, reliable, well-grounded, competent and mature beyond her years.

Not at all the kind of person love happened to.

If she was honest—and now that she had her moment of clarity, there was no going back to lying to herself—it had happened the first time she had seen Blake.

The look in his eyes, the set of his shoulders, the tilt of his chin, the smile that had lit his face when little Dorothy Andrews had brought him a rock she had painstakingly painted. It had happened right then.

Determined not to be ruled by her newfound realization, nor to be terrified by it, Holly turned from the mirror, added a few logs to the fire that was sputtering and marched back to her chair.

She looked at her agenda, flicked open the computer file for transfer documents, and typed in the first name on her list.

Her heart felt like it was going to explode inside her chest, and her face felt like it was on fire.

She squinted at what she had typed.

Dismayed, she read the very thought that had come to her with such startling clarity when a knife held at her throat had made her face her deepest secret and her strongest yearning, her soul telling her what would make her life complete.

Instead of the name Clifford Drier, she had typed, *I am in love with my boss.*

She stared at it. She highlighted it to erase with her delete button, and instead managed to put it in bold print.

I am in love with my boss.

Ridiculous, that she, a paragon of responsible secretarial behavior, would write such a thing, nurse such a childish and unprofessional crush. Ridiculous that she would believe she had loved him from their first meeting. As if love could happen that fast!

Everybody loved him. The kids loved him. The staff loved him. The benefactors, especially Joe Colton and his beautiful wife, Meredith, loved him. She'd have to get in line to love Blake Fallon!

She went to insert a bold *not* in between ''am'' and ''in.''

The line magically deleted, as if it had never been.

Two

Blake climbed in his ranch vehicle, a brand-new silver-gray Nissan Pathfinder that had been donated to the ranch recently by Springer Petroleum. A surprising donation, authorized by Todd Lamb, who had replaced David Corbett as vice president of Springer after Corbett had been arrested for poisoning the water.

A premature arrest as it turned out, to the surprise of no one who knew Corbett. Blake, whose skills at judging people had been honed to razor fineness because of a childhood that required a number of interesting survival skills, including the ability to read people quickly and accurately, had suspected they had the wrong man.

But he had been wrong many times, too, most notably when Joe Colton had come to his rescue, after a judge had decided that was one motorcycle too many that Blake had helped himself to. An angry young teen at the time, Blake had nearly been bitter enough to not listen to the voice deep within him that had told him, loud and clear, *this man you can trust.*

Joe just had never given up on him. Ever.

Since then, Blake had learned to listen a little better to that voice that whispered within him. It helped, especially, in dealing with these kids. Kids who had learned to lie and cheat and steal when most kids were learning their alphabet. Blake could tell in a glance if a child was lying—and why. There were so many motivations, and few of them had anything to do with the kid being bad. Self-preservation and fear were the two that usually headed the list.

He could also tell if it was a tortured, unexpressed sadness that had motivated an act of vandalism, or a need for attention, or just plain old garden-variety belligerence.

So, when he'd first heard David Corbett had been arrested, he'd told his pal Rafe James his thoughts on the subject. Short and sweet. No way it was Corbett.

Rafe came from the mean streets, too. He read people as well as Blake did, maybe better. The happy ending to David's tragic false accusation was that Rafe was a changed man—the quintessential lone wolf's heart had been warmed by David's fiery daughter, Libby.

The thing that struck Blake as odd about Todd Lamb having Springer donate the vehicle to the ranch was that it was the type of thing David Corbett might have instigated, but not Todd. David, on the few social occasions when they had met, had always impressed Blake as being open, generous, authentically kind. It had been such a relief when David's name had been cleared and he'd been let out of jail. Always a man determined to find reason in all the events of his life, David said the whole incident had propelled him toward doing what he really wanted to do with his life. He'd retired. Still, if the culprit was not David it did mean that a very dangerous individual, one capable of harming children, one who had tossed the dice with human lives, was still on the loose out there.

Todd Lamb, on the other hand, whom Blake had also met at the odd ranch fund-raiser or at Colton social functions, seemed to be cold, ruthless and ambitious. Not the kind of man who would give away a vehicle without a string attached.

The vehicle had come with the official explanation that Springer knew what an incredible inconvenience the residents and staff had been put to because of the ranch being evacuated. The official letter said that though they claimed no responsibility even though the chemical found in the water, DMBE, was used by them, as a responsible corporate citizen they hoped to be of assistance by offering extra and reliable transportation while kids were still being ferried around the countryside as a result of the contaminated water.

Blake's first conclusion had been that Holly must have gone to Todd, her father, and asked him to help out. She'd had to put a lot of miles on the old ranch vehicle, a minivan that had probably been the prototype for minivans, but when he'd asked her, Holly had looked as surprised as he by her father's generosity.

It seemed incongruous that she could have sprung

from the same tree as Todd Lamb. Though Blake detected a slight physical resemblance between the father and daughter, that seemed to be where all similarity ended. Holly had qualities of warmth and gentleness and integrity that shone right through those convent-approved suits she wore.

In just eight months, Blake was amazed how absolutely indispensable she had become to him. How her presence had changed the whole office.

Her predecessor, Mrs. Bartholomew, had been a battleship in pink polyester. Efficient, yes. Pleasant, no. The kids had been terrified of her. She called it respect. He might have been a little terrified of her himself, though he'd done his best never to let it show—another trick of an old street fighter.

Certainly the whole ranch staff seemed to have sighed a big sigh of relief when she had announced her retirement.

And then Holly had come. His office was in a lovely old white clapboard ranch house that had been converted. He had a simple apartment upstairs, which the downstairs served as office space for the Hope-chest Ranch.

Holly had loved the house on sight.

"Oh," she'd said dreamily, of the outer office, "this used to be the front parlor of this house."

He'd seen a certain gleam in her eye when she investigated the old river rock fireplace that seemed so out of place among filing cabinets and her desk, and the government office reject chairs lined up against the walls for kids who were in the office having paperwork done or were waiting to see him.

Soon she had a fire crackling away in that hearth

every single day. The kids loved it, and the older ones lined up for the opportunity to chop and haul wood for her.

Then her desk had been pushed back into a corner, and the ugly metal frame green and orange vinyl chairs had disappeared. From somewhere she'd found an old blue sofa that she'd put a bright plaid throw over, and several wingback chairs which she had grouped around the fireplace.

An old trunk served as a coffee table, and it always had a heap of comic books, coloring books and crayons on it. She had hung lace valances on the tall old windows, and their wide casings held an assortment of plants that the children clamored to water.

A huge round fishbowl with four residents of various colors and fin shapes had a place on top of her filing cabinet. Standing on a chair to sprinkle feed for the fish seemed to be a special honor reserved for newcomers who arrived confused, frightened and tearstained.

Often the quiet murmur of voices drew him out of his office and he would find her, work stopped, having a quick snuggle on the couch with a needy child.

With something approaching reverence she took the artwork the children had made, and while they watched, she would pop it into a cheap frame and hang it on a bare spot on the wall. One whole wall, floor to ceiling, was nearly completely covered with these bright testaments to the resiliency of the human spirit.

The only pictures that had hung on the walls before were the worker's compensation posters that Mrs. Bartholomew had put up religiously. As if she was in any danger of falling off a ladder, or being backed over by a truck. Pretty hard to miss something that big in that shade of pink. But if someone had hit her with a truck, he had the uncharitable thought it was the truck that would have needed repairing, not Mrs. B., as she had reluctantly permitted herself to be called.

"What are you going to do when you run out of walls?" he'd teased Holly one day.

"Run out of walls?" she'd said, astounded. "We have a whole ranch."

Somehow having every wall on the whole ranch hung with the kids' colorful drawings appealed to him very much.

"Where are you getting the frames from? You're not buying them yourself, are you?"

She'd shrugged.

He'd quietly arranged for the downtown hardware store to donate a hundred frames. When that box arrived, she'd oohed and aahed like it was Christmas morning and he had given her diamonds.

The truth is he probably would have kept Holly even if not a lick of the office work got done. She attracted the kids, and she was good with them. She had, seemingly effortlessly, turned the dull space of her office into an area of good cheer and happiness, a place that it felt good to spend time in.

He even found himself wandering out there to get a handful of those little butterscotch candies she kept, and to sit on the couch in front of the fire and visit with whatever kid was on her sofa for the afternoon.

But, amazingly, she still got the office work done with incredible accuracy and efficiency. Her mind was exceedingly quick, not rigid and slow moving as her predecessor's had been.

It was Holly who had first mentioned the water as a possible source when a terrifying number of kids had first started getting sick at Hopechest. And then everybody was sick. Her mind had sorted through information to the common denominator with breathtaking quickness. He credited her with the fact that the situation had never been allowed the opportunity to deteriorate into a terrible tragedy.

And though Holly Lamb was nothing to look at, she was a huge step up from Mrs. Bartholomew. She always looked presentable and professional and to Blake's abject relief she had yet to wear pink. And every now and then he would notice her eyes behind those huge glasses, and try and figure out what color they were.

Some days he would be convinced they were blue. And the next day he would decide they were brown.

His office had changed in the most subtle and pleasant ways since her arrival, and he was already keeping his fingers crossed that she would never, ever quit.

Hard, though, to think of her as Todd Lamb's daughter. He wondered what her mother was like.

And then he remembered the expression on Holly's face when he had first come through the office door today.

It had troubled him then and it troubled him again now. When he had asked her what was wrong, she'd laughed it off and tried to turn it into a joke, but the expression on her face had been downright strange.

He shot a look at the boy sitting sullenly beside

him in the passenger seat. He knew that look anywhere. Guilt. His instinct told him the boy could tell
him all about that look on Holly's face if he was
approached in the right way.

"So," Blake said, looking straight ahead at the
road, "where are you coming from?" Out of the corner of his eye he caught the slight hunching of thin
shoulders.

The boy hesitated, and then muttered the name of
a juvenile detention facility.

"Oh, yeah," Blake said. "I saw the inside of that
one once or twice myself when I was your age."

Startled surprise, quickly masked. "Sure."

"No kidding."

"What for?"

"I took motorcycles that didn't belong to me."

"Cool."

Blake decided to let that pass, and he knew better
than to pry about what the kid had done. He could
find out later if it interested him.

"When did you get out?"

"A couple of weeks ago. I tried to find my sister.
I promised."

"Yeah. She told us."

"I was supposed to go to a foster home when I got
out, but I'll be sixteen in a few weeks, so I figured
I'd take a miss."

Under the nonchalant expression, Blake heard the
question. Am I in trouble?

"I'll find out for you," he said, just as if the question had been asked out loud.

The boy gave him a surprised look.

"How come my secretary looked so strange when

I walked in?'' There. He'd given him something, now he wanted something back.

The boy took a sudden interest in his sneakers, then his fingernails, then the scenery outside the windows.

''I dunno.'' His eyes were skittering around like crazy.

A lie. Blake gave him the look that said he knew it was a lie, and the boy tried to do a turtle and pull his head inside his own jacket.

A long silence ensued, which Blake did nothing to break.

''I was really mad. And scared. And tired. It was a dumb thing to do.'' The voice was coming from somewhere inside the jean jacket.

''What was a dumb thing to do?''

''Pulling the blade on her.''

Blake, who prided himself on being unshockable, on keeping his cool in any circumstance, swerved the vehicle onto the shoulder and braked to a halt so fast that the boy's head popped out of his jacket.

''You did what?'' It registered, somewhere in him, that this was not *him,* the unflappable Blake Fallon. But the thought of someone scaring his sweet secretary filled him with a quiet and protective rage that did not bode well for the boy sitting next to him.

Tomas shrank back against the door. His hand moved stealthily for the handle. ''Don't hit me,'' he whispered.

And Blake snapped back to reality. He took a deep breath and tried not to think of Holly on the end of a knife.

''I don't hit kids,'' he said quietly. ''Nobody here hits kids.'' Given the paleness of the boy's face, he

decided to skip the lecture on the possible conse-
quences of pulling a knife on someone. If it had been
his old secretary, that boy would be in cuffs already,
on his way back to where he'd just come from.

But instead of that making him appreciate her
more, Blake suddenly felt furious with Holly for putting him in this situation. He'd asked her what was
going on, and she'd lied to him. Maybe, he admitted,
he felt furious with her because for a moment pure
emotion ruled him.

"I didn't see a knife when I arrived at the office,"
he said, putting the vehicle back in gear and pulling
back onto the highway.

"She kicked it under the desk when you came in."

Great. He felt his ire rising again. Not only had she
lied to him, she'd deliberately misled him.

"Do you have any more weapons on you?"

"No."

"Do I have to check?"

"No."

He glanced at Tomas, and saw truth there. He arrived at Hacienda de Alegria, Joe and Meredith Colton's lavish ranch, and shook his head. There were
kids everywhere, spilling across the lawns and out of
the big sprawling house that dominated the scene.

Meredith Colton, who really should have been enjoying her retirement, was running frantically with a
homemade kite, kids on all sides of her, running and
laughing, their faces lifted to the sun.

Joe had a little fat pony saddled and a small girl
had a death grip on the saddle horn and a huge smile
on her face as Joe led her around the yard. Another

dozen or so kids were hopping along on either side of them, excited to have a turn.

Blake shook his head. He'd been worried about imposing on his foster parents when they had offered to take the kids from Hopechest. But when the logistics of keeping the ranch open by bringing in water and supplying bottled water for drinking had proved impossible, he had accepted their gracious offer.

He realized now he had never seen two people look less imposed upon. The pair of them looked like they were in all their glory.

"What is this place?" Tomas asked, his eyes wide, his nose pressed to the window.

"It's a temporary home for the kids who were displaced from the ranch."

"No kidding?" he breathed. "I kind of imagined heaven looking like this."

"That's kind of how I felt when I first saw it, too," Blake confessed. Tomas was way ahead of where Blake had been, though, if he could admit something like that. Blake, at that age, would have considered such an admission soft.

A half hour later Tomas had been reunited with his sister, and Joe, with his knack for trusting those who had never been trusted, had put Tomas in charge of pony rides.

"What's his story?" Joe asked quietly, as he and Blake sat on comfortable cushions on the bent willow chairs in the deep shade of the porch.

"I don't know yet," Blake said, taking a sip of his iced tea. Just the way he liked it. Tea and lemon, no sugar. Trust Meredith to be watching the sugar intake of all these kids. "I just found out from him he pulled a knife on my secretary."

"Really?" Joe said mildly. "Surprised he has any teeth left."

"I don't hit kids."

"Well, none of them ever pulled a knife on Holly before. Meredith and I are very taken with that girl."

Holly was making several trips a week between Hacienda de Alegria and the Hopechest Ranch with paperwork. But Blake suspected many of her trips were just because she missed the kids so much.

He did, too.

He noticed a twinkle in Joe Colton's eye that seemed to encourage a confession that Blake, too, was quite taken with his new secretary.

Blake had a desperate need to deny it. "I would have been ticked if it happened to anybody, and not enough to be smashing heads, either."

"Well, maybe you wouldn't have been that ticked if it had happened to Mrs. Bartholomew," Joe guessed.

Blake had to chuckle. "Okay, maybe not her. Joe, I don't have any kind of interest in Holly Lamb, aside from the fact she's the most wonderful secretary I've ever had."

Joe looked skeptical.

"For God's sake, it would be totally unprofessional."

"I don't recall saying a word about your relationship with Holly, professional or otherwise. But let an old man share some wisdom with you."

"Do you have to?"

"Yes. She's the kind of girl men pass up. She

doesn't catch the eye, like a piece of tinfoil in the gutter. She's more like gold. Gold doesn't shine much when you first find it. You have to look hard for it.''

"I'm not involved with my secretary. And I don't plan to be. Joe, I have an example to set. My behavior has to be exemplary in every way.''

"Who are you trying to convince you're perfect— the rest of the world or yourself? You've got to quit lining up those paper clips in neat rows and live a little.''

An annoying statement, uncomfortably close to the one Rory had made recently. Something insulting about him polishing his stapler.

Of course, Rory was all buoyance and light and unpolished staplers now that Cupid's arrow had found him.

Joe could still make Blake feel like an awkward kid, still ask all the right questions.

He also knew precisely when to drop something.

"Look, Meredith and I have set our party for a week from Saturday. We think its about time to have some fun.''

Blake looked at the three-ring circus happening around him and wondered glumly how much more fun it could get.

"This whole thing has been terrible on the morale of the whole town. We're going to have a good old-fashioned barn dance. Get people laughing again, give these kids a chance to see there are wholesome ways to have fun. Can I count on you to come?''

"Oh, yeah, like you need me to have fun.'' Blake had an independent nature that did not lend itself well to social functions, which he detested. His job required him to attend some, but he rarely attended any voluntarily.

"I don't *need* you, but I sure like it when you're around, Blake. You know Meredith and I consider you as much our son as Rand and Drake. Meredith wants you to come, too. Plus, of course, it would be setting a good example to your staff, showing them it's time for a change in mood, time to move forward."

"I'd feel better about doing that when whoever is behind the contamination of the water system is found."

"Maybe he'll never be found," Joe said. "It's important to move forward now, past the fear and tensions of the last couple of months. You can poison kids like these without ever touching their water."

"He'll be found," Blake said. "I won't rest until he's found. Sinclair from the FBI, and Rafe feel the same way."

Joe nodded. "Well, since we've got the three of you on it, the rest of us might as well start relaxing, hmm?"

Blake grinned. "Okay, I get your point."

"Good. Are you going to come?"

"Okay. I'll come," he agreed reluctantly.

"Feel free to bring somebody with you."

Blake squinted at Joe suspiciously, but there was not a flicker in the older man's face to suggest he thought that someone should be Holly Lamb. As if.

"Can Tomas stay here for a day or two? Until I find out where he's supposed to be, and if he needs to go back?"

"Oh, sure," Joe said easily as if one more kid was a joy.

That was what Blake had felt here, for the very first time in his life. That his presence in this universe was a joy to someone, instead of a burden.

"Well, don't forget he pulled the knife."

"Blake, look at him. He hasn't let go of his little sister's hand since he arrived. He's been helping snotty-nosed kids on and off that pony for the better part of half an hour. I like the cut of his jib."

"Well, you always see it first, Joe."

"Don't I?" Joe said happily. "Go home and make sure that secretary of yours is okay. Though she looks to me like the kind of girl who would know just how to handle a scrawny, scared kid with a knife."

Blake thought of coming into the office, Tomas weeping against Holly's slender shoulder, and he sighed heavily.

"I suppose you like the cut of her jib, too."

"You said it first, not me."

Three

Holly knew, as soon as she heard the crunch of the Pathfinder's tires on the gravel outside the office door that, in some part of her that she would much rather not acknowledge, she had been listening for it to return, waiting for the moment Blake would stride back through the door, smile at her, maybe stop to talk for a few minutes about his day and the developments in the water contamination case.

The vehicle door closed quietly, not like their old vehicle that had required a good hard slam. The Pathfinder itself still troubled her. The gesture seemed so unlike her father. It was not that he wasn't generous—she'd received dozens of expensive gifts from him. Or at least the cards were signed by him.

The gifts themselves had his secretary, Hannah's demure personality written all over them. Holly suspected her birthday was penciled right on Hannah's calendar, not her father's. Which was probably why she felt odd about the gift of the Pathfinder.

Todd Lamb was not thoughtful. Or sensitive. He was not even particularly astute about the good public relations move. He had been reprimanded more than once for making anti Native American remarks.

He was a man who had risen to a high position in Springer because he was smart, tough and ambitious. Her father had told her once, with great pride, that he was the kind of man every company wanted. He could turn one dollar into ten, and he didn't care whom he ran over to do it. Why would a man who took pride in turning one dollar into ten, insist on repainting the nearly new Springer vehicle from perfectly acceptable white to silver gray?

Not knowing why, Holly shuddered, then put the whole thing out of her mind. She busied herself with the typing, when the door swung open.

She glanced up at just the right moment, and smiled cordially at Blake when he came through the door. The smile hid more than it revealed.

For instance, you would think, after you had seen a man a certain number of times, the novelty of him would wear off.

That you would no longer notice the color of his eyes, the little Dennis-the-Menace rooster tail in his hair, the powerful shape of his shoulders, the easy and effortless ripple of his arm muscles.

You would think, after a while, that the loose, graceful swing of his walk wouldn't make butterflies take off in your stomach, and that you would be able to look at his lips without wondering what they tasted like and what they would feel like, and if you were ever, ever going to know.

She realized she had been having these thoughts for a long, long time. The crush on the boss wasn't new, just her admission of it.

He was so handsome. She loved his eyes. She felt like she could look at him forever. She had the awful thought her newly discovered feelings were going to be in her face, that she would stumble over her tongue now, turn red whenever he spoke to her.

Diligently, she looked back at her work, began to type furious nonsense, which she hoped at least wouldn't say she was in love with her boss.

When he neither greeted her nor went by her into his own office, she glanced up, to see him perched on the corner of her desk, one leg swinging, the other anchored to the floor. He looked at her thoughtfully, his brow furrowed. His normal smile, the one that put the sun to shame, was nowhere in sight.

He looked distinctly…crabby.

"Anything you want to tell me about?" he asked.

She swallowed. No. Even he wasn't *that* intuitive, though he was dangerously alert to undercurrents and unspoken things going on all around him.

He shocked the kids with this uncanny ability to look into their hearts.

Ralph, you got something in that pocket I should know about?

Shirley, anything happen last night you care to share with me?

Polly, do you need to talk to me?

And as it turned out Ralph had a joint in his pocket, and Shirley tearfully admitted to escaping from her second-floor dorm window and running across the roof to peek in the boys' dorm, and Polly had been keeping a kitten under her bed that had turned seriously ill.

But Holly didn't have any secrets of that nature. Secrets that had witnesses or hard evidence.

How much could he read into a blush, a stammer, a quick lowering of eyes, after all?

"Something to tell you?" she said, pleased with how smooth her voice sounded, just as if she was the same person as she had been when she arrived at work this morning, when in fact she was changed in some way that was so fundamental she knew she could never change back.

"You know. Some interesting detail about your day." His you-can-confide-in-me voice invited trust, showed genuine interest.

She stared at him, flabbergasted, and resisted the urge to pinch herself. Was he actually showing interest in her personally? It seemed too much to hope for, following so closely on her discovery of the feelings she was harboring in the far and secret reaches of her heart.

Her golden opportunity. To make him smile. To make him *see* her. All she had to do was think of something clever, or funny, or interesting to share with him about her day.

Not one single thing came to her mind.

She had always performed terribly under pressure. She knew if she was ever chosen to play Wheel of Fortune, she would be one of those people who asked for a letter that had already been used.

"Well?" he said silkily, leaning toward her, something glinting gravely in his eyes.

"Willie died," she blurted out.

"Willie?"

"The guppie."

"A fish?" He looked stunned, like he didn't have a clue what she was talking about, and why should he?

A golden opportunity, blown. She said miserably, "The one named after the whale. As in *Free Willie*."

He said nothing.

"I'll go get another one tomorrow," she babbled. "Little Flo Henderson was very attached to him."

"Anything else you want to tell me about? Aside from the unfortunate demise of Willie?"

It occurred to her there was something pointed about his question. That he wasn't expressing a nice generic kind of interest in her. He was probing for something specific.

Annoyed at herself for hoping too much, and at him for not even being in the same ball park as her, she said crisply, "If there's something specific you want to know, you'll have to tell me. I don't do well at twenty questions."

"How's this for specific—"

It occurred to her the glint in his eye that she had mistaken for interest was actually anger. Blake was angry at her.

"—what does it feel like to have the blade of a knife pressed against your pretty little throat?"

"Oh," she said, deflated, "that." She wondered if it counted at all that Blake Fallon thought her throat was pretty.

"Oh, *that*. Hardly worth mentioning."

"To be quite frank, I'd forgotten about it already."

"It seems to me I asked you if something was wrong as soon as I stepped into this office and saw you with Tomas. It doesn't seem to me as if I got a straight answer."

"The whole thing was already long over by the time you got here."

"Oh? The way I heard it, the knife was being shoved under the desk by your big toe just as I came in the door. Is it still there, or did Miss Efficient file it already?"

Miss Efficient? "Actually, I did file it already. It's in the trash. Outside."

"Not inside, where I might see it."

She was beginning to feel really angry. This was what his interest in her was about? The first strong emotion he had ever shown to her was annoyance? Anger? She realized she had not totally forgiven him yet for that teasing but still slightly stinging remark he had made earlier.

I didn't know you were a girl.

And now the brief interest that had lit in his eyes was about this? Even his remark about her neck had been accompanied by that cynical tone of voice.

"I had no interest in hiding the knife from you," she said stiffly. "I put it in the outside garbage so I didn't have to see it every time I disposed of a piece of paper."

"Meaning the episode did leave some impression on you."

"Some," she agreed reluctantly.

He leaned very close to her. "In the future, if you

are attacked by someone with a knife, do you think it would be asking too much to let me know?"

"I explained to you, it was already over. And it was nothing. I never really felt threatened. I never even really felt frightened."

"And you didn't want to get him in trouble," he guessed softly.

"Now that you mention it, I didn't want to get him into trouble."

"Your first loyalty belongs to me, Miss Lamb."

Now she was really angry. "No, it does not, Mr. Fallon. It belongs to me. You seem quite satisfied with my heart telling me what to do with these kids so far. Tomas wasn't a dangerous boy, he was a frightened one."

"And if you had a few years experience with these kids, instead of a few months, you would know that was the most dangerous kind of all."

She could see he was angry, too. Really angry for the first time since she had been employed by him. She had never even seen him get irritated with the children, but now his voice had a dangerous edge to it, and his eyes were snapping with sparks that had not the slightest thing to do with passion.

She sighed inwardly, but not out loud. Wasn't that just her luck? Discover the humiliating secret that you were madly in love with a man who was never even going to give you a second look, and then end up in his doghouse on the very same day!

"If that's all, Mr. Fallon," she said, looking at her watch, "I really should have gone home half an hour ago."

Her voice was perfect. Reprimand accepted. Except

then she went and spoiled it all. Her lip trembled just a little bit. She ducked her head, but not quickly enough.

The silence filled the room. She refused to look at him.

His hand found her chin and lifted it, and she was forced to look at him. She saw the immediate remorse flash through the gray depths of his eyes.

"I've hurt your feelings."

"Not at all," she said. Her voice was trembling now, too. It would have been so much better if he didn't touch her, if his hand was not resting on her chin, his fingertips leathery and tough. Yet his touch was not tough at all. It was everything she had known it would be.

Electric. Strong. Tender.

"Here you are, working extra time, as always, and I come in and blast you."

His cold, hard anger was much, much easier to handle.

"You were absolutely right, I should have told you about the knife. I just didn't even think. It won't—"

"Holly, I think what I should have said was that it scared me. When Tomas told me what had happened, I could imagine you at the end of that knife and it scared the living daylights right out of me."

She stared at him. He was not a man who looked like anything would scare him. She had seen him face tough, angry kids, big kids, without even a flicker of fear. So what did that mean, that he had been scared for her?

"I'm sorry it happened to you," he said in a low voice.

Don't read too much into it, she warned herself. He would have been sorry it happened to anybody. He ran a tight ship. An incident had occurred out of the far reaches of his control. His fear for her had not been personal.

"I guess what I wanted to say was that I don't want you siding with the kids against me," he continued. "I need to know what's going on, and I need to know you trust me."

"Oh."

Now that he was being nice, she felt more like crying than ever.

"Maybe," she whispered, "I need to know you trust me, too."

"Oh."

He let go of her chin, thankfully, though her skin felt like it burned where he had touched it. He leaned back and ran his hand through his hair. The rooster tail sprang right back up the instant his hand passed over it.

"You know what?" he said.

She shook her head mutely. Too much to hope that he was going to say, I just realized I'm madly in love with you.

"We've been working too hard," he said instead. "The whole water thing has put an incredible amount of stress on the ranch, and you and I have been carrying the majority of the load. I know you've been putting in more time in the front lines than anyone could have asked of you."

This was looking hopeful. You and I, as in a partnership.

"Joe Colton was right. He told me he thinks it's time to move on."

"That would be a whole lot easier if the culprit had been caught."

"That's what I said. When I spoke to Kade Lummus today, he said they have a firm suspect. That's very confidential."

She knew it was his way of telling her he did trust her. "But he didn't tell you who?"

"No. I took Rory out for lunch after, but I'm afraid I couldn't even use our old college friendship to get that out of him. Not even for the secret fraternity handshake."

His quick sense of humor was coming through again. It was almost as if nothing happened. They slipped so naturally back into the easy give-and-take that had become a hallmark of their relationship.

After they had discussed the water a little further, she told him she had pulled Lucille's file and put it on his desk, as she thought he might need it to figure out what to do about the sudden and probably totally unauthorized arrival of her brother, Tomas.

"He's going to stay with Joe and Meredith for now," Blake told her. "I'll have to do some checking and see what kind of trouble he's in, but really I think—knife aside—he just wants to be with his sister. I'll see what I can do for him."

"You don't believe he's dangerous, either."

"Let's not go there again."

She grinned, relieved that the old tone seemed to be back between them, realizing how much she looked forward to her communication with this man, how much a part of her life he had become.

In fact, the Hopechest Ranch now seemed to be her whole life, much to her father's disgust.

"Your brains and your skills and you're working as a secretary? For a pittance?" Todd Lamb never passed up an opportunity to belittle her efforts.

Well, maybe she was kidding herself, but somehow she felt like more than a secretary. She felt like she mattered, and that these kids needed her. For the first time in her life, someone needed her.

Her relief at the old tone being back between her and Blake was pitifully short-lived.

"Joe told me he and Meredith are going to host a barn dance a week from Saturday to try and lighten the mood in the community, bring people together again. He's got this funny idea that people are more good than bad, given a chance, and that the folks of Prosperino need to be brought back to that wholesome truth."

She ignored Blake's slightly cynical tone. "What a charming idea. Honestly, Joe and Meredith Colton are such a lovely couple." The kind of couple she envied so much. The kind of couple who had found it. That thing that everyone searched for.

Love.

Found it and let it sustain them, but more, had not just kept it as sustenance for themselves and their family, but had given it away over and over again.

To the community, to their foster children.

And in that giving, they lived a truth that the whole world needed to know: that love given away, multiplied itself and came back.

Holly suddenly felt so lonely she thought she might cry, after all. She'd never had that in her own family.

Her mother was totally self-involved in her looks and her shape and her clubs, and her father was totally self-involved in his career and his power plays. They were two people with no time for each other, and in the end, no time for their daughter, who had needed things from them so desperately.

"Holly?"

She looked up, forced herself to smile. "Hmm?"

"You looked so sad for a second there."

"Oh," she said. "I think you were right. Too many things have happened. It's been very stressful. You may have even been right about the incident with the knife. It may have made more of an impression than I thought."

"You're in need of some diversion."

"I have a great book at home." She wished she could snatch that back the moment it slipped out of her mouth. Good grief, she sounded like a pathetic old maid. It was a good thing she hadn't mentioned her cat, as well.

"I had something else in mind," Blake said. "Why don't you allow me to take you to the dance? As a way of thanking you for all the extra work you do, and apologizing for being such a boor right now."

She understood then that their relationship could never go back to what it had been before. Not now that she was carrying the secret. If she didn't love him, it wouldn't have mattered that he had only asked her out as a way of saying thank-you. Or apologizing. Or because he felt sorry for her.

Even with her new secret knowledge, or maybe because of it, she had some pride.

Her handsome boss fully expected his plain-Jane

secretary to fall all over herself with gratitude because he had asked her out.

Methodically, not meeting his eyes, she turned off her computer and neatly covered it with the dust cover. She placed her paperwork in a neat stack, and when she was totally composed she gave him a steady look and a frosty smile.

"Let me think about it," she said, and was rewarded with the stunned look that appeared on his features.

She suspected no one had ever said no to Blake Fallon before. Oh, she'd seen how all the beautiful women of Prosperino fawned over him.

Well, it certainly wouldn't hurt him to feel what the rest of the world felt for once.

She took her pocketbook out of the bottom drawer of her desk and shrugged back into her neat navy jacket, then stood up.

"Excuse me," she said coolly.

He couldn't get off the edge of her desk fast enough. She suspected he was still watching her, his mouth open, as she went out the door.

But she didn't give him the satisfaction of looking back, even though she suspected he stood in the office doorway, watching her as she walked all the way home.

Home was only a few hundred yards from the office, a lovely little cabin that had once served as a bunkhouse on the ranch.

Her mother and father, had they taken the time to visit her here, would have been mortified by her humble lodgings. She was a long way from the palatial home outside of Prosperino that her mother and father had once shared and that she had grown-up in.

But as she walked up her creaking steps, she felt a wonderful sense of homecoming. The cat, Mr. Rogers, woke up from his favored position on the rocking chair on the front porch and came to greet her, rubbing himself against her legs until the static crackled.

"So it's you who's responsible for the hair I always have on the seat of my pants," she greeted him. She realized if anyone was watching, talking to her cat would make her seem even more the pathetic old-maid secretary.

So she bent down to pet him, taking a quick glance back over her shoulder at the office. She had been wrong. The door was firmly shut, and Blake was not watching her.

As if.

She opened the door to her cabin and went in, and the troubles of the day seemed to fall away.

She loved this space she had made for herself. Some of her favorite drawings from the children were on the rustic log walls, pictures of the children themselves crowded her mantel. The rough wood floors that demanded slippers at all times were covered in bright throw rugs.

Her simple furniture—two red plaid armchairs and a yellow love seat—were shaped in a semicircle around the fireplace. The same stonemason must have done all the ranch fireplaces, because they were all equally beautiful.

A ball of wool attached to two needles, which a

sweater had been taking shape out of for the last six months, was heaped on one of the chairs.

There was a stack of romance novels under the coffee table—a new addiction, one she now could see was quite related to her feelings for her boss. It was a safe way to explore her feelings without making a fool of herself.

The way she would have if she had said yes to his invitation to accompany him to the dance.

She wandered through to her bright but small kitchen, put her purse on the table and traded her shoes for her slippers.

Of course, she reminded herself, she hadn't exactly said no, either.

She had said she would think about it, and true to her word that's exactly what she was doing.

The lovely feeling of homecoming dissipated, and it occurred to her that of course she was going to say yes. Eventually.

With a moan of something approaching terror, she went into her bedroom. It was another room that gave her great pleasure, a peaceful feeling. Her big four-poster bed with the white eyelet lace cover and pillows provided such a beautiful contrast to the rough-hewn gray logs of the walls. It was a room that would have looked in place a hundred years ago. It was a restful space.

And that restfulness was completely lost on her.

She threw open her closet door and began to sort frantically through the meager items hanging there. After realizing she had not one suitable thing to wear to a barn dance or any other kind of dance, she went into her tiny bathroom and looked in the mirror.

She took off her glasses and studied her eyes. Hesitating, she reached for a small pot of makeup.

An hour later she stared at herself, aghast. She looked precisely like Bobo the Clown.

She found herself making the call she never thought she would make.

"Mom? I need you."

Four

$\mathbf{B}$lake lay awake and restless in his bed until he could stand it no more. He hadn't had a decent night's sleep in weeks. He would lie down, and the horror of all those people getting sick would start to replay in his mind. Especially the kids. The fear in their eyes. The paleness of their skin. Running the first ones to the hospital in the old van. Then the old yellow school bus. And then the ambulances coming, one after another.

Rationally he knew it wasn't his fault.

Irrationally, he believed it was his job to look after them, and that he had failed, just like everyone else most of these kids had ever placed their trust in.

The helpless fury came then. Who would hurt children? Especially ones like these, who had already been hurt so damned much by life?

After punching the pillow a few more times, and getting his legs tangled up in the covers, he finally got up. The room had a distinct chill in it, so he pulled on his jeans, then flipped on the light. His bedroom, like his office, was free of clutter, and had about as much character as a barracks. Metal frame bed, gray blankets, white sheets. Clothes folded neatly on the chair underneath the window. Somehow those rooms had been vastly preferable to the constant bickering of his mother and father when they had been together. After they had split, his home life had deteriorated even more. He knew with that razor-edged intuition of children, that neither of his parents wanted him. He put a cramp in his mother's manhunt, his father was cold and indifferent. Blake came to wear the label worn by so many children in pain: incorrigible.

These were the kind of rooms he had come to manhood in. Plain, no frills foster home bedrooms and detention center dorms.

Then he'd arrived at the Coltons'. Meredith had delighted in making a room just for him, asking him subtle questions about his favorite colors and his favorite sports, leading him up the stairs one day and throwing open the door of a room he had never seen before.

"This is for you," she'd said.

Just for him, a bedroom that had been every boy's dream. She'd tactfully overlooked his interest in motorcycles, which had been the cause of most of his grief, and decorated in a baseball motif. The walls were covered in baseball posters, and there were matching blue, red and white curtains and quilt. She had found him a signed Joe DiMaggio ball and put it in a glass case. The bat, which had hit a winning run in a California Angels game that Joe Colton had taken him to, was signed by the team and mounted on one wall. There had been a desk and a computer and a stereo and a study lamp.

But the truth was, he'd been sixteen when the Coltons took him in, and his tastes were already formed. He felt at home with a certain monkish austerity, or maybe deep inside himself he did not believe he deserved all the fuss, did not quite believe he would ever be the kind of wholesome all-American boy who would fit in a room like that one.

Brushing aside the memories, Blake went out to his kitchen and flipped on a light. There was paperwork all over the table that he had wanted to get to tonight, but even though he couldn't sleep he didn't want to do it now.

His decorating theme of no-personality repeated itself in this room. It looked like a kitchen in an empty apartment. Except for the papers on the Formica table, it was a barren landscape. No canisters on the counters, no magnets on the fridge, one little soup stain on the stove the only evidence someone actually lived here.

Out his window, he could see the ranch and all its buildings. Emily's House for the young unwed mothers, the Homestead that lodged temporary residents, kids waiting for fostering or adoption or to go home, and the Shack, a halfway house for juvenile delinquents. There was a school and a gymnasium and an art studio. In the center of the buildings was a green area and baseball diamond, and on the outer rim of the ranch were barns and corrals and fields and pastures.

He might have allowed himself a moment's pride, since much of this had been his doing, but the ranch seemed unbearably uninhabited, like a ghost town. Even the livestock had been moved because it would have been far too expensive to start trucking in water for cattle and horses.

His eyes were drawn across the roadway to Holly's little cabin. In the window boxes her red geraniums were gilded silver by moonlight. The cat was enjoying the rocking chair on the porch. It looked like the kind of homey scene someone with some artistic talent might want to capture. Cat in a Rocking Chair at Midnight.

He looked for any shadow of movement, the ranch grounds bathed in the soft orange of the yard lights they had installed just last week, in case whoever poisoned the water came back to finish the job they had started.

He shook his head, not wanting to get back on the merry-go-round of fury and helplessness.

He gazed instead at the darkened windows of her cabin and bet her kitchen didn't look like this.

Come to think of it, he didn't really want to think about her either.

He opened his fridge and inspected the contents. One carton of milk of dubious age. One package of cheese which had not been that shade of green and blue when he had originally purchased it. Mustard and ketchup, neither of which he thought would make a very appetizing sandwich on its own. In the crisper were two withered apples and a package of slime that he deduced had once contained lettuce.

He glanced out the window again and told his mind firmly not to go there.

It went anyway, right into her fridge, where there would be neat rows of delicious and healthy things to eat. Fresh milk, cream for her coffee, oranges and apples and pineapple spears, maybe a neatly packaged leftover chicken potpie or tuna casserole. She probably had chocolate chips to make cookies, and lard to make pies.

"Or maybe her fridge looks exactly like this one," he told himself.

This preoccupation with food was a brand-new one. When the kids were in residence the camp cook fed him along with everyone else and didn't mind him scrounging through the fridge for leftovers in the middle of the night. He loved Dagwood sandwiches, and seeing how many things he could squish between two slices of bread. Whole pickles, thick slices of beef, jalapeño peppers, tomatoes.

His mouth watering, he opened his freezer compartment. The Häagen-Dazs was at the very center of a frigid cave of thick, wavy ice.

"There is a God," he muttered, and took it out. He lifted the lid, and inspected the intricate and frosty crystals that had formed on the surface. He knew trying it was the act of a desperate man, but he got a spoon, and hazarded chipping into the ice cream. He tasted, paused, smiled.

He wandered into his living room and sat on the sofa. It was expensive black leather, not particularly comfortable. Tonight it felt cold to lean his bare back against it. He had a chrome and glass coffee table, which he put his feet up on.

"Decorations by Harley," he decided, looking around critically. Maybe he hadn't ever really put his penchant for motorcycles behind him. This was what being tired did—made a man's mind go places it didn't generally go.

And tonight his apartment seemed to him a lonely place. Without personality and without soul.

Not to mention cold.

Abruptly, he got up, feeling as if he was being pulled by a magnet. He went down the narrow stairs to the office below. There was only ash left from Holly's fire, so he carefully rebuilt it, enjoying the ritual of shaving kindling, lighting the match, blowing the embers to life, feeding in progressively larger wood. He liked his fires man-sized, not like those little piddly things she lit.

By the time he had the fire roaring, his ice cream was nearly melted, but he settled himself on her sofa, the afghan over it warming his bare back, and sighed with something that dangerously approached contentment. It was cozy down here.

But difficult as hell not to think about her when it was all her little touches that made this room so much nicer than the one directly above it.

The truth was he couldn't believe Holly Lamb had told him she'd think about allowing him to escort her to the Coltons' dance. That was almost a no.

From her. Miss Mousey.

What had he expected? The truth? He'd expected her to fall all over herself saying yes, because that's what women, in his experience, did.

Women with a hell of a lot more on the go than her. Looks. Sophistication. Polish. Great bodies.

He did not look at this assessment in the light of being conceited, it was just his experience of reality. He asked women out, they said yes. Women liked him. Beautiful women liked him. It had driven his roommates in college crazy, before they'd begun to twist it to their advantage.

"Invite Fallon along. He's a babe magnet. Great leftovers."

He'd come to take it somewhat for granted. Sometimes it even irritated him, how persistent some women could be once he'd shown the tiniest bit of interest.

The truth was that Blake always harbored the thought that the interest of the coeds would have waned fairly quickly if they'd known the whole story. If they'd had any idea how often, before his sixteenth birthday, he'd had his hands cuffed behind his back.

Only Joe and Meredith, and a few really good friends like Rafe knew. Rory now, too, since he had run a mandatory background check on all the staff at the ranch when the water system had been contaminated.

Rory had been amazed. "Mr. Straight-A-don't-leave-the-hair-in-the-hairbrush-in-my-bathroom stole motorcycles? Who would have guessed?"

"Believe it or not," Blake had said drily, "those experiences have helped me do my job here a hell of a lot more than the MBA."

But something must have flickered in his face, because Rory had added hastily, "Don't worry. It's a juvenile record. It's sealed."

Of course, it had come unsealed quickly enough when the FBI wanted it.

No sir, Blake hadn't let any of that side of himself show at college. Not even to his roommate. He didn't even drink, for fear that that wild side was just waiting to get back out, betray those who had taken a chance and believed in him.

He let some of it show now, on select occasions, when he used his own dark history to get past the defenses of kids who knew some of those same feelings: the dread of hearing those words: "Get your hands up where I can see them." Or "Get on your face *now*." Or "Up against the wall. Spread 'em." Kids who knew the feeling of manacles too tight, the pat-down, the lonely, hopeless click of the cell door locking.

Once, when he'd been about fifteen, he'd taken a stolen bike on a wild ride up the coast, and made it all the way to Washington State before he got caught. On probation already, he'd been flown back to California under escort on a regularly scheduled commercial flight. He still felt sick when he thought of the look on the stewardess's face, the young mother across the aisle keeping her wide-eyed toddler away from him, the indifference of the sheriff who wouldn't even remove the cuffs to let him eat the meal. His first time ever in an airplane. Scared and defiant and humiliated.

Once you had those kinds of experiences, they were a part of you forever.

No, the girls who had followed him around campus, and phoned him and fallen all over themselves to say yes if he asked them to go for a coffee, or a game of pool, or anything else, hadn't ever suspected that side of him. No, instead they'd actually looked at *him* with their dreams of picket fences and golden retrievers and strollers dancing in their eyes.

For some reason, his mind went directly to Holly. He thought of coming into the office to find her holding that boy today. A boy who looked like he hadn't had a bath in a few weeks and who had just finished holding a knife to her throat. Loving him anyway. Seeing his heart. Not the least bit concerned about that boy's past.

Of course, she was not in the same league as the kind of girls who had chased him around campus. She was that fade-into-the-background kind of girl. The kind that hid in the study carrels at the library and walked around with huge stacks of books covering her chest. No form-fitting sweaters, cute little skirts that twitched when she walked, no practiced coy looks, or pouting lips. No skipping classes to ride around in patched-together convertibles, no getting a little tipsy and giggly as those first beers passed over virgin lips.

Virgin lips.

Now he was wondering, very inappropriately, if she was a virgin.

Was he suddenly intrigued by his little secretary because she was the first woman he could ever remember not falling all over herself to say yes to him?

Oh, no, she who looked like she had never been on a date in her entire life had looked him up and down coolly and said with great composure, she would *think* about going out with him. What was her expectation? That tomorrow he was going to ask her if she'd thought about it and what her answer was? That he was going to beg her? That he was going to think of nothing else until he had her answer?

The sad truth was he hadn't been thinking of much else.

Maybe she preferred nerds.

Was that a possibility? That a nerd could be preferred over him? Someone like the little banker who had just moved into town? Glasses, bow tie, three-piece suits, polished black shoes.

No memories of cell doors closing, of course.

He was crumpling his empty Häagen-Dazs container in his bare hands, crushing it actually. The container had really done nothing to deserve such violence. He threw it in the fire and watched morosely as it took flame.

Not that she'd been a complete Miss Mouse this afternoon. When the anger had flashed in her eyes, he had realized they were the most astonishing shade of green. He'd realized, behind those glasses, her eyes were large and shaped like almonds. He'd realized—

Every muscle in his body bunched up as he heard the handle on the outer door tried.

He froze for a second, and then leapt panther-light to his feet. He hoped it was whoever had poisoned the water. He hoped to God it was. He had a lot of frustration built up inside of him, and it had been a long, long time since he had been in a situation where it would be socially acceptable to vent a bit of it by crashing his fist into a face.

The door swung open, and he didn't know which of them was more surprised.

"Oh," Holly said, "I'm sorry. I didn't realize it

was you. I saw the fire flickering from my window, and I thought I better come check. You know, I thought whoever poisoned the water might be in here—''

"So you just flew right over to check? By yourself?"

Her hair was down. He'd never seen it down before. It was long and smooth and touched her shoulders. In the firelight, it looked like honey in a jar, with sun streaming through it.

It was almost enough to diffuse the annoyance he felt with her. Still he had to ask. "What the hell did you think you were going to do if you had come across an arsonist lighting the place on fire?"

"Oh, you know," she said, "after you've wrestled a knife from a junior assailant you feel ready for anything."

The remark totally disarmed him.

Then, from behind her back, she pulled a baseball bat. It was so incongruous, the thought of her going after anyone with a bat, that he laughed. And then she laughed, too.

Their eyes met and held, but she looked away first.

"Well, good night," she said, and turned swiftly back into the night.

"Wait, Holly, come in for a second."

She stopped, threw him a questioning look over her shoulder.

"Uh, I just wondered if you were having trouble sleeping."

She held his gaze, and took one small step back into the room. What was so different about her? The hair, of course, but something else.

"A bit," she admitted. "The ranch seems so empty, so wrong, somehow. Everything feels spooky. And I can't figure out if I'm being paranoid when every snapping twig seems like a bogeyman, or if I'm being realistic. Somehow I needed to come over here and face my fear, instead of shivering, terrified, behind the door in my cabin."

He hadn't thought of her being frightened on the empty ranch at night. In the office she seemed so competent, so in control. It occurred to him maybe he should have thought that a woman by herself in the vicinity where a despicable crime had been committed—a crime that could have easily killed many, many people—would most likely be afraid. Terrified.

"Maybe you should move to town."

She looked offended.

"Do you want some cocoa?" he asked, suddenly Mr. Sensitive. Better late than never.

She hesitated, while he wondered what the hell he was doing. He had just told Joe this afternoon that his behavior had to be exemplary in every way. He doubted if that included entertaining a woman who worked for him, who was under his authority, in front of his fire after midnight. When he was bare-chested, and the top snap of his jeans undone.

Trying not to draw attention to himself, relying on the dimness of the room, he reached down and snapped the rivet shut. Naturally, it sounded like a gun going off.

Was she blushing? Was there anyone left in this world who was that innocent? It was really hard to tell, since the light from the fire flickered and leapt and died and then leapt again. He bet she was a virgin.

Still, he excused himself, he'd offered her cocoa. That was quite different than offering her coffee spiked with Kahlua or a shot of Jack Daniels. His plan was to offer her a bit of company and comfort, not to seduce her.

"Sure," she said after a moment, "a cup of cocoa would be nice."

Having put forward the invitation, he suddenly wondered if he had cocoa, and doubted it. He suspected she'd read his mind, because a small smile played across her lips.

"I'll just run across to the kitchen building and get some," he said.

"There's hot chocolate here. I keep it for the kids. Do you want me to put the kettle on, while you, um, go find a shirt?"

She was embarrassed that he didn't have a shirt on, which he supposed was ample evidence there were people left who were that innocent.

She moved into the room, avoiding looking at his naked chest, and he realized what was so different about her tonight. She was wearing blue jeans, not a skirt. And a red sweatshirt that had the Hopechest letters and logo emblazoned across the front of it.

He had always hated the name Hopechest for the ranch. He thought it far too feminine, and didn't like the picture that formed in his mind of an eager young woman stacking linens and ornaments and china in a chest, her head full of completely unrealistic and romantic notions.

He thought the kind of kids who wound up here

had a different take on life than that. Radically different.

But the name was historical, given to the ranch by the first blushing bride who had lived here in the late eighteen hundreds. And who had probably died of cholera or in childbirth or something equally gritty.

Still, history was history, and the Board had unanimously vetoed his suggestion to rename the ranch the Hopechest Ranch, even though he had so persuasively pointed out it would only mean a change in one letter, and he didn't mind doing it by hand on his own business cards and stationery.

It was Holly who had changed his mind about the name.

He'd been mumbling his various complaints and dissatisfactions about it one day, and she had stopped him short.

"It's a perfect name," she'd said firmly. "A hope chest isn't just about getting married. It's about hopes and dreams and a belief in the future. A good future. It's about beginning to put the things away that you need to make that future become a reality. Isn't that exactly what this ranch is about? Teaching these kids the skills they need so that they can believe in the future, begin to harbor hopes and dreams for themselves that they never dared to harbor before?"

And he'd had no answer, and found himself not minding the name so much since then.

Now, seeing it emblazoned across *her* chest, it seemed like it could be given another twist on hope, altogether. He was sure his prim secretary would have slapped his face if he'd shared that with her. The sweatshirt, the little bow from her pajamas peeking over the V, showed him the surprising fact that Holly Lamb was quite curvy.

The jeans, too, hugged her slender legs and caressed the curve of a thigh and hip he had never noticed before. She turned at the fire and bent over it, picked up the poker.

Now how had she managed to hide that asset from him for eight months? Somehow he reined in his thoughts and headed up his stairs at a dead gallop.

When he came back down, she was curled up on the couch, her feet tucked under her, her hands wrapped around a mug, gazing at the fire.

"Your hot chocolate is over here," she said, gesturing toward the end table on the other side of the sofa.

One couch. Two of them. Perhaps it would be safer to sit in one of the wing chairs that flanked the fireplace. But his mind refused to process the directive. It was preoccupied by the question of her innocence or lack thereof.

He sat down on the other end of the couch, and made himself look at the fire instead of her. Mostly. Every now and then he'd take a quick peek.

No glasses tonight. Was that an incredible cheekbone or a trick of light? And how could her eyes be gold? This afternoon he'd sworn they were green.

"How come you can't sleep?" she asked.

"I've had problems with insomnia ever since it happened. The water. I lie awake at night and torture myself with what-ifs. What if I had reacted more slowly? More quickly? What if I caught whoever did it? What if I don't catch whoever did it?"

She just nodded. She didn't try to solve it. She

didn't giggle or toss her hair over her shoulder. She just was.

And he realized, suddenly, he didn't feel as lonely as he had ten minutes ago.

"Have you thought about going to the dance?" he heard himself asking. No, it couldn't be him. He had vowed he wasn't saying one more word about that stupid dance. Vowed.

She turned and looked at him, full in the face.

It was the firelight that had made him ask again, he realized. It was playing all kinds of tricks with her plain features, playing tricks with his mind.

"Yes," she said.

He ordered himself not to pursue it. Let her come to him. His mind mutinied, disobeyed his orders blithely. "Yes, you've thought about it, or yes, you are going to go with me?"

She looked back at the fire. She looked very composed. For a minute he thought she was going to make him pursue it *again.*

But then he saw the small pulse beating in the hollow of her throat, and it reminded him of a frightened rabbit. He knew frightened things. He knew one false move and they bounded away. He sat very still.

She said, finally, "Both. Yes to both."

And he felt the oddest sensation—happiness.

Five

Holly looked at the document she was keying with dismay. She, the world's most notorious perfectionist, was making mistakes. All kinds of mistakes. Two names jumped out at her that were spelled incorrectly. In paragraph four she had transposed numbers. She *never* transposed numbers.

Of course, the typos were the least of her errors, easily wiped out with a quick backspace or delete.

Her other mistakes were less easy to fix.

Starting with the mistake of asking her mother for a little help in the makeup department. She'd told her mother she would take the weekend and go there, to her mother's upscale condo in San Francisco, but the rapidity with which that offer was refused clued Holly in that there was probably a new man in residence. She could just guess: graying hair, distinguished fit and, of course, fabulously wealthy.

Totally unaware that her youthful-looking mother had a twenty-seven-year-old daughter.

And under all that polish he'd be a jerk, just like the last one. And the one before that. He'd have a secret penchant for the bottle, or a mistress stashed in every major city across the U.S.A. and Canada.

Now, because of that teeny mistake—asking her mother for help—her mother was coming here for the weekend, arriving tomorrow, Saturday, morning.

Here. Where she'd laugh at Holly's cabin, sneeze at her cat, make embarrassing eyes at Blake if he had the misfortune to be around, and worst of all endlessly bemoan the bone structure and looks that Holly had not inherited from her.

What moment of insanity had made her call her mother? Oh, yes. Looking at the makeup job she had attempted on herself, in preparation for saying yes, as if Blake Fallon had asked her to marry him, and not to a simple dance. That "yes" was another in the chain of mistakes that she was not able to fix.

But while her mother might be a pain, when it came down to it, Rose Lamb Jones Andover Bennet knew everything there was to know about making a woman look beautiful. Even if that woman was the daughter she had called Plain Jane to her face all her life.

Her mother had actually sounded delighted at the invitation. Couldn't wait, were her exact words, as if she had been holding on breathlessly for Holly to come around to her way of seeing things all of their shared lives.

But the mistake of calling her mother paled in relation to the biggest mistake of all. The biggest mistake of all had been crossing the road that separated her quarters from Blake's the other night.

Really, if she would have known what she was going to encounter she would have let the building burn to the ground. The whole ranch.

Anything would have been better than standing there in the flickering light, watching the gold and red licks of flame reflect off the masculine perfection of his naked chest.

Of course she had seen things like that before. On posters. In magazine ads. In movies, on TV. What shocked her how unprepared she was for the pure potency of a man half-dressed at close range.

Which brought her to the final mistake of her mistake-riddled life.

Why had she ever let herself admit she loved him?

It was like a weakness that flowed through her veins now instead of blood, especially that night, gazing helplessly at the play of light across muscle and skin, his unclothed upper body a beautiful and breathtaking array of taut bulges and hard ripples.

All of which she had wanted to touch.

Instead, she had managed to squeak, like a girl straight out of the convent, that she thought he should go put a shirt on. When of course she thought no such thing. Her real thoughts were so wanton that she felt a stranger to herself.

A stranger she liked. A stranger who might have proclaimed the room way too hot, which it had been with that stupidly large fire he had built, and might have removed an article or two of clothing herself. A stranger who might have let him know, with a wink or a look, that she wanted to know what his lips tasted like, what his hands felt like, what it would feel like to be caught tight in the hard banded steel of his embrace.

She looked at what she was typing and gasped. "Head-on" had become something quite different. She backspaced over it and thoroughly checked the rest of her document for Freudian slips.

Anyway, somehow she had escaped that night with her dignity intact.

And her virginity. But she'd vowed right then and there it was going to be him or no one. Another mistake, because it committed her more to her course with her mother.

She probably had him to thank for not losing her head.

He had stayed on his side of the couch. He had not made one improper move or suggestion. They had drunk cocoa instead of mulled wine or Spanish coffee. One glance from him, one crook of his finger, and she would have cast herself on him like a jezebel.

There was the awful truth of it.

She wanted him desperately, madly, badly, insanely.

And he had finished his cocoa in what seemed to be one long gulp, and then offered to walk her home and not listened when she had told him that wasn't necessary at all.

As he had walked her back across the road, she had allowed herself the fantasy that he would pause in the darkness of her porch and see her.

Really see her.

He'd see her integrity, the goodness of her heart and her intelligence and he would love her for all those things. He would take her in his arms, and touch his lips lightly to her lips and then harder, until they were being swept away on a tide of passion, his heart recognizing all that was real and wonderful about her, even if his eyes had misled him into presuming she was the dowdy and efficient secretary.

Had she read the faintest surprise in his expression about something that night? What? The no glasses? The hair down? Why would that surprise him? She knew it really didn't help. She should know by now men didn't see her.

She was still plain. What's more she didn't play the game. Her mother's game. Power through beauty. Holly called it the debutante mentality. Still, if she'd agreed to that coming-out party over a decade ago, she'd probably know how to put on her own makeup by now.

No, there was no use kidding herself. The interest was one-sided, and now she had to live with the discomfort of working side by side with him when she had a secret that he would likely never share.

When she was leaning closer to get a whiff of that soap-and-sunshine scent that was all his, he was just pointing out a sentence he wanted changed in a letter.

It had been absolute hell getting through this week. He had not even referred to that cozy moment on the couch—except to tell her the Coltons had confirmed a time for their dance for one week this Saturday. A barn dance theme. Dress western.

At least he hadn't tried to squirm out of his offer to take her. Yet.

"Hello, darling."

Holly looked up with dread. What was her mother

doing here already? It was only Friday. She was supposed to come tomorrow morning.

"Hello, Mother."

Her mother, under the impeccable makeup, looked suspiciously like she had been crying. Which meant the new relationship was going about as well as the others, and explained the early arrival. Rose was a silvery shade of blond this week, and still a perfect size four. The pantsuit looked like an Armani, and the bag and shoes Gucci.

She certainly did not look old enough to have a daughter Holly's age.

She was regarding Holly, one long tapered fingernail, which matched her stunning pink silk outfit to a tee, pressed against the side of her mouth.

"I can see why you needed a little help. Goodness, what is that you're wearing?"

"I'm fine, thanks, Mother. And how are you?" She sighed. "It's a suit, Mom. This is what people wear to offices."

"A suit? It doesn't look like a Chanel or a Dior."

"It's a Wal-Mart."

Her mother looked like someone had passed wind in public. "Really, darling, if you need money, you know I've always been more than—"

"Mom, I'm twenty-seven years old. I take a certain amount of pride in the fact I can make it on my own."

"Oh. Well, that's refreshing, dear."

Holly was quickly covering her computer, hoping to get out of here before Blake's office door opened and he came out. On the one or two rare occasions she had brought boys home to meet her mother, Rose had stolen the show with ease, and Holly had had to spend the rest of the night with people who seemed more interested in her mother than her.

"I'm just about ready to go. I'll just pop in and get these papers signed and tell Blake I'm leaving a few minutes early."

"Your office is so quaint. What did you say you do here? Orphans, isn't it?"

"Something like that."

"Where are the little darlings?"

Her mother despised children nearly as much as she despised cats.

"Mom, I told you. There was an awful, um, accident here. Involving the water."

"Oh, of course, I do remember you telling me that. I'm sorry. It was right before I left for Monte Carlo."

Holly wondered if her mother would have canceled her trip if Holly were one of the ones who had gotten so sick she needed to be hospitalized. It was the kind of question she had nearly driven herself crazy asking as a child.

She got up from her desk, aware of her mother looking with horror at the neat black skirt and double-breasted jacket Holly had thought was so professional-looking this morning.

"You know, darling, just a silk scarf would have done wonders for that outfit. Red and white and black."

Trying not to sigh too heavily, Holly tapped lightly on Blake's door and went in, pressing the door firmly closed behind her, and leaning on it for a moment.

"Something wrong, Holly?"

"Er, no."

"Last time you told me that you'd just finished having a knife pressed to your throat."

"This is only slightly worse. My mother."

"Didn't you say she was supposed to arrive tomorrow?"

"My mother is always full of unexpected surprises. She's early."

"Look, do you want a few extra days off? You certainly deserve it."

She stared at him in horror. Extra days with her mother? She wasn't even sure how she was going to get through this weekend.

"I'll take that as a no," he said drily.

She pulled herself together and moved away from the door. "I'll just get you to sign the Bonner letter before I go. And the transfer for Jamie Lynn Barker. I'll go get her and bring her to the Coltons. I just spoke to Meredith—" the woman every person wished was their mother— "and she said—"

She saw his eyes widen, and knew without turning around her mother was in the mysteriously opened doorway of his office.

She turned and sure enough, Rose stood there with a mollified smile on her face as if she had accidentally leaned on the door and it had just opened.

"Oh," Rose said. "You must be Holly's boss. I've heard so much about you. I've just been dying to meet you."

Blake's name had never come up in a conversation between Holly and her mother, not even when she had told her she needed a little make-over assistance.

"Mr...." Rose was coming forward, her hand regally extended, as if she were the queen.

"Fallon," Holly filled in. "Mom, my boss, Blake Fallon. Blake, my mother, Rose Lamb. I mean Rose—" She fumbled for the last husband's name.

"Bennet," her mother filled in smoothly, giving Holly the tiniest sour look.

"A pleasure," Blake said, rising and coming around his desk. But something in his voice made Holly turn back and give him a quick look.

For heaven's sake. This had to be a first in human history. He did not look the least bit taken with her mother. He was not grinning at her with that frank male approval Rose had spent her entire life perfecting how to get.

He took her hand, shook it and let go.

"My," Rose said, blinking up at him, "what a powerful handshake you have, Mr. Fallon."

Holly cringed and looked for a place to drop through the floor. Did her mother have to flirt with everyone? Couldn't her daughter's boss be off-limits?

"Thank you," he said. "I developed it lifting weights while incarcerated."

Holly sent him a shocked look, then noted her mother's quickly faltering smile as she backed steadily for the door. Suddenly, Holly felt like laughing.

"I'll wait for you outside, dear," her mother said frostily. She looked like she was going to take a hanky out of her purse and wipe her hand.

When the door had shut behind her mother, she faced him.

"I'm sorry," he said. "You didn't know, did you?"

She was trying not to laugh. Really, this was very

serious business. Her boss had just trusted her with a very important fact about his personal life. Of course, he couldn't be too sensitive about it, since he had used it to deliberately shock her mother.

A little snicker slipped out of her. And then she laughed. "I'm sorry, Blake," she sputtered, "but the look on her face! Why did you say that?"

"I don't know," he said with a careless shrug. "There's something about the color pink that makes me see red."

"I'll remember that," she said, wiping her eyes.

"See that you do, Miss Lamb." He leaned the back of his legs against the front of his desk, and folded his arms over his chest.

"I will, Mr. Fallon."

"Do you care?" he surprised her by asking, his look suddenly intense.

"About the color pink?" she asked, flabbergasted.

He laughed. "No. That I spent part of my youth under lock and key."

She regarded him somberly, and the words came from so deep within her, it felt like her soul speaking.

"Of course, I care," she said. "I wish nothing bad had ever happened to you. But I see it as a mark of who you are, that you turned your greatest tragedy into your greatest asset. That you can use your experiences to make a difference in the lives of these kids is a wonderful thing. Maybe even a miraculous thing.

"Blake Fallon," she said, almost fiercely, "I know exactly who you are."

He looked at her for a long time before he smiled,

slow and soft and sweet. "And that's the difference between you and your mother."

Why did she feel like, even though he had revealed a secret about himself, it was her secrets that were dangerously close to being revealed?

"You know when I met your father, I assumed you must take after your mother. But now that I've met her, I realize you take after the best person of all."

"Who is that?" she asked, loving the mood in the room, the almost intimate feel of it, and wishing she could hole up in here forever, bask in his approval.

"Yourself. I think you are one hundred percent yourself, Holly, and that is the rarest of things."

Considering she was about to alter that self to win a little something more than these brotherly feelings, she didn't know what to say.

He surprised her by leaning forward, and gently pushing the glasses up on her nose. "Thanks for saying that, Holly, about my tragedies becoming my assets. I hadn't ever quite seen it in that perspective."

His hands dropped to his sides, and he returned behind his desk. He didn't look back up at her, already engrossed in whatever was before him.

"Enjoy your weekend," he said as she opened the door and went out.

Her mother was waiting, perched on the edge of the sofa as if she thought she might get dirty from it.

She got up and came and looped her arm through Holly's. "Really," she said in an undertone. "How can you stand working for that awful man?"

"Some days it's harder than others," Holly admitted. Of course, Blake had been relegated to her mother's "awful" pile because he had failed to fall all over himself over Rose.

"Incarcerated," Rose said with a sniff. "I can't imagine you knowing those kinds of people. How on earth would he get a job? What do you suppose he did?"

Holly led them out the door, and they crossed the street.

"I have no idea. It doesn't matter to me." Somehow she didn't feel the least inclined to share with her mother it was a juvenile record—possibly because she knew that wouldn't make much difference to her mother.

"Well, I care! I will not have my daughter working for an axe murderer."

"Did he strike you as an axe murderer?" Holly asked drily.

"Well, er, no, but then you know my judgment in men is terrible. Look at your father."

Holly decided to change the subject, holding tight to Blake's words. *You take after the best person of all.* It felt like the loveliest of compliments, something she could use like armor against her mother's barbs and disapproval and judgments.

"Well, this is where I live."

Her mother stopped and stared at the little cabin. "Oh, my. I would have mistaken it for a tool shed."

"I'm going to make you chicken tetrazzini for supper," Holly said, bravely, naming her mother's favorite. She opened the door to her house, and the cat hurtled out the door like a rocket. Mr. Rogers was intuitive to dislike.

Rose stepped inside and began to sneeze.

Two hours later, Rose had Holly captive in front of the makeup mirror she had brought with her.

"Now, first it's the eyebrows. Dear, they are just so heavy. Really, the shape of your eyebrows sets the tone for your entire face. Do you want them heavy and unruly, or do you want them light and graceful and feminine?"

"Feminine," Holly muttered.

With what seemed to be a certain amount of sadistic pleasure, her mother located her eyebrow tweezers in a huge bag she had brought.

The first hair was plucked out, and it was Holly's turn to sneeze. "Not too many," she said, feeling suddenly trapped and panicky.

"Trust me," Rose said smoothly.

But Holly thought it was probably a little too late for that. Still, when her mother proudly let her look in the mirror at her newly shaped eyebrows, she was surprised by how much more delicate her whole face looked, feminine. Nearly pretty.

"See?" her mother said. "Now, the main event." She was looking eagerly through her bags, bringing out an amazing array of creams and colors, makeup brushes and lipstick tubes.

Watching her, Holly realized her mother was glowing. This was what she loved to do. She felt a little pang that she had never seen that before. That when her mother had pestered her about her looks, she had really been trying to share a part of herself with her daughter, struggling to find common ground.

In her way, maybe her always wanting to interfere with the way Holly looked had been her way of trying to say she loved her.

If she accepted her mother being here as a gift of love, as Rose knew how to express it, it changed everything.

"Mom, what I need is for you to show me how to do it. I can't have you do it for me, because you won't be here all the time. And," she said gently, "it has to be my style, not yours. I want to look natural."

"Good makeup always looks natural," her mother said with a sniff. "But I understand what you're saying. We have all weekend. We'll come up with what's right for you. I promise."

Within a short time, they were giggling like schoolgirls, as Holly fumbled with the unfamiliar mascara wand. Holly could not remember ever sharing moments like this with her mother.

An hour later, Holly looked at the completed effort in the mirror. She bit her lower lip. She didn't really look changed in any way. But features she didn't know she had were suddenly glowing in a soft spotlight.

Her eyes in particular looked wide and deep, the color of them amazingly highlighted so that they looked very, very green tonight. The minor blotches and blemishes had miraculously disappeared from her complexion, and her skin looked soft and creamy. She actually had cheekbones, and they were high and beautifully showed off the shape of her slender face. Her lips looked full and wet, like lips that were waiting to be kissed.

"You see," Rose said, "I always tried to tell you. You don't have true beauty. Your looks come from your father's side of the family. Speaking of your father, have you heard from him lately?"

"Oh, he calls from time to time to tell me I'm throwing my life away. Last time he called, he told me he had been making some investments that were about to pay off in the millions." Holly didn't tell her mother about the edge in his voice that she had found deeply disturbing.

"He called me several weeks ago, too," Rose said. "He sounded quite agitated, not himself somehow. He told me I could quit looking for a rich husband. Soon he was going to have enough money that he wouldn't mind throwing a few crumbs my way."

Holly felt the hairs on the back of her neck rise, but before she could wonder why, her mother continued.

"He always had a tendency to be so crass. Oh well. Let's not worry about him. Despite his contribution to your genetic pool, you have some very attractive features, and your eyes are truly amazing. You need to wear your hair down, because the shape of your head is too blocky, and that softens it. I'd see a hairdresser if I were you. You need some highlights. Your hair! Your father's again. Terribly drab."

Well, drab would not do.

"By the way, who's the man?"

"Pardon?" Holly drew her eyes reluctantly away from the mirror.

"A woman doesn't take a sudden interest in her looks without a man in the picture."

"Oh, really, no, there isn't." She didn't know if it made her sad or glad that her mother did not pair her with her boss, did not even think it might be him.

"Well, whoever it is, he's a lucky man," Rose said, and kissed her on the top of her head. "I really don't know how two such horribly self-centered people as your father and I managed to raise a daughter like you. You're sweet, Holly.''

Holly didn't know what to say. She felt like she was going to cry. Thankfully, the phone rang. It was the juvenile center wondering if someone could come for Jamie Lynn tonight as they had a sudden urgent need for the bed.

To her surprise, her mother said she would come with her to get the girl.

They dropped off Jamie Lynn at the Coltons', her mother suitably impressed with the obvious wealth of the estate. She would have loved to meet Meredith and Joe, but they weren't in that evening.

''You know,'' she decided suddenly, when they arrived back at Holly's cabin, ''I think I'll stay at a hotel tonight. I can't imagine what I'll look like in the morning if I sleep in that cabin with all the cat hair. My eyes get puffy. And I think I'll just head on home in the morning. You don't mind, do you?''

When had anything with her mother ever gone the way she expected it? Had she secretly hoped they might have a few more giggles together, a moment or two more of closeness? Holly suspected those were the very things that were scaring her mother away.

''Not at all. Thanks, Mom. You really do know how to make a woman look her best.''

''Don't I though? I would have loved to get my hands on that girl we drove from the center. Poor thing. Did you see the eyeliner?''

She was packing her makeup lovingly back in a bag, but left a neat row of items on the table. ''This is what looked good on you. I'll leave these here.''

"Thanks, Mom. I can't say I noticed Jamie Lynn's eyeliner."

"Well, other people will, and it's a bad start in life. Some doors will be closed to her before she even has a chance. Maybe you didn't notice her eyeliner particularly, but you probably did notice she looked cheap and hard, all because of terrible makeup, and those frightful clothes, that awful dye in her hair.

"Well, ta-da dear. Call if you need anything." And with that her mother was gone.

Six

That you can use your experiences to make a difference in the lives of these kids is a wonderful thing. Maybe even a miraculous thing.

Her words kept coming back to him, making him view his life in quite a different way, making him think differently.

Blake was in his office. Not the place everyone would choose to be Saturday morning at seven o'clock, but what the heck. He'd never caught on to golf.

Still, the work kept fading, he couldn't focus on it. The question kept coming back.

Did he believe his life had been in any way miraculous? That all of his life meant something and that he was part of a larger plan?

A nice thing to believe. Naive, but nice. Hopelessly

optimistic, but nice. In a way, that was what Holly had been doing since she got here. Making things nice, taking the hard angles and coldness out of his world and replacing it with her warmth, her soft touch everywhere.

He wondered about miracles, a subject he knew nothing about. What if there was a quota, and he'd used his all up? He could think of a number of things that, in retrospect, if looked at in that softer light, might qualify as a miracle.

When he was fifteen he'd opened up a stolen motorbike full bore on a highway slick with black ice. He'd lost it in a corner, and the bike had slid out from underneath him, and he'd gone skidding across the highway like a surfer on a wave—except his body had been the board. Not a scratch.

Then there was the time he and one of those dubious characters he'd called a friend back then had been swiping stereos out of cars on a nice quiet residential street and the dog squad had showed up. They said it couldn't be done, but Blake had outrun the dogs. His buddy wasn't so lucky, and was still scarred from the twenty-six stitches it had taken to close his leg.

He couldn't count the number of times in his life that he'd had his back against the wall, been outnumbered and outpowered, and still managed to come out of it with his head high.

They were not exactly the kind of situations one expected miracles in, nor had he ever been the kind of guy who expected to get them. And yet, looking back now, he felt the smallest little niggle of wonder. Maybe. Maybe they had been after all.

And of course there was one bona fide miracle in his life, even if the others didn't quite qualify. Joe Colton taking an interest in him, insisting on seeing qualities in him he could not see in himself. Joe believing it so implacably, Blake had come to believe, too. That he was worth something. That was a genuine miracle for a boy who'd been shuffled between his estranged mother and father like an unwanted pet.

His desperate need for affection unmet, he'd learned to settle for attention. At least when he was in trouble, his parents acknowledged he was alive. Blake remembered his mother coming to retrieve him from jail the first time. Her face had been white she was so livid. She'd been at an afternoon card party. There had been an interesting gentleman there. How could Blake do this to her? What if people found out? Of course, the more she cared about people finding out, the more he didn't. He began to take a certain pride in his renegade reputation. In the end, that backfired too and he wound up in foster care, and graduated to the thrill of stealing motorbikes, at first just for the joy of it, and later for profit. Eventually, he ended up being on pretty intimate terms with most of the juvenile detention facilities in Northern California.

Over the years now he'd watched other kids get on that same train he'd gotten on, kids driven by desperation and fear and anger and frustration. They didn't always get off where he had. No mansion on the country estate for them.

Nope, all their cards ended up reading ''Go straight to jail. Do not pass go.''

So, he'd already had his fair share of miracles, now

that Holly had him thinking along those lines. Had he used them up?

He needed one more. Desperately.

He needed to get those kids back on this ranch. They needed him, just as once he had needed Joe. This ranch was one way of stopping the train, at least for some of them, that train of despair and hopelessness they had gotten on way too young.

They needed to be here. They needed the structure and the security. Blake needed to get them back so he could start all over again. Make them feel safe. Like the world cared about them.

A much harder task now that some of them had been poisoned.

He tried to get his mind on more practical matters. He was reviewing job applications for a new counselor to replace Celia Walters who was getting married, but his mind kept wanting to wander back to miracles.

Not one kid or member of his staff had died from that water.

That was a miracle.

And here was one of a fairly major nature: how a barracuda like Rose Bennet had produced Holly. In fact, Holly's father struck Blake as pretty predatory, too. A shark and a barracuda—out comes a guppy. Impossible. Incredible.

He heard the outer office door whisper open, and went out of his own office.

Her hair was down again today, falling like a curtain over her face as she tried to get her sticky key out of the lock. Her hair was golden and fluid, shimmering with light. It made him think maybe he'd made a mistake. Not a guppie, after all. Maybe a goldfish.

"Hi," he said. She had on a neatly pressed white blouse and a pair of navy trousers, sensible flat shoes. It was probably her idea of casual, since it was Saturday.

She looked up, startled. "Oh, hi."

"You forget something?"

"No, uh, I just came in because Jamie Lynn was released last night and I wanted to call her grandmother and let her know she's okay."

"I'll do it. It's your day off. Go golfing with your mom."

"I don't golf."

Well, that was a point in her favor.

"Take her shopping or something, then. There's a new restaurant open in Prosperino. The Red Herring. Supposed to be good."

"The truth is, Blake, my mom left earlier than planned."

She ducked her head and moved by him to her desk. He dealt with enough kids whose parents had hurt them to know she was disappointed. And he'd known her for long enough now to know she wasn't going to let on.

Interesting. Yesterday she had said that to him, *Blake Fallon, I know exactly who you are.* Now he felt the same way about her. There was a refreshing honesty between them now that he knew who she was.

And right now she was hurt, and didn't want him to know.

He thought of asking her if she wanted to go to

The Red Herring for lunch with him. But maybe that wasn't such a good idea. Asking her to the dance had been enough of a mistake.

Because ever since he'd done that there had been this funny little awkwardness between them. Nothing big. Nothing he could even put his finger on. Just something there that hadn't been there before.

He missed what they'd had before. A kind of companionship, respect, trust, an easy camaraderie and flow to their relationship.

That was why you didn't mix business with pleasure. That simple. Still, he couldn't leave her trying so hard to look brave, like she didn't care if her mother had left practically before she had even gotten here.

This was the truth about mothers. Kids loved them. They loved them if they were junkies. They loved them if they were liars. They loved them if they broke every promise they ever made. They loved them if they were incapable of putting the needs of their children ahead of their own. They loved them, and believed every single word they said. If a mother said the world was made of blue cheese, then that was so.

And what did these children ask as a reward for their love and devotion and loyalty? Nothing. But somewhere in this secret place deep within them, they wanted to be loved back.

Sometimes by people who could not do that.

He knew that was true if the kid was three or thirteen or thirty-three.

He knew it was true of Holly, and he searched his mind for some small thing to make her pain less.

"Your hair looks nice like that."

She touched it self-consciously, did not look at him. She whipped the cover off her computer as if a national emergency required her immediate attention.

"Oh," she said, "that's what my mother said. She said it helped my head not look so blocky."

Blake had a sudden urge to throttle someone. He could even imagine his hands wrapped around Rose Bennet's wrinkle-free-by-surgery neck and squeezing until her eyes bulged.

It was the kind of urge that he had relegated to his former life, that he liked to believe he had long ago left behind.

The urge faded by itself as he watched Holly turn on her computer and stare resolutely at the screen. The urge shifted shapes unexpectedly, blindsiding him. It became an urge to hold her, to make it all right. To tell her her inner beauty was what mattered.

She had said to him, "I know who you are," as if she could see his heart and soul.

And he felt like he could see hers for a moment. A wonderful moment, when she met his eyes, and he saw that hers looked brown today, deep, kind, troubled.

"You know, Holly," he said awkwardly, "you're twice as beautiful as your mother, without half trying."

She stared at him, stunned. The most interesting shade of red was creeping up her cheeks. There. Sir Galahad had embarrassed her instead of helping out.

"On the inside," he said hastily, "where it counts."

And then he could have kicked himself, because it sounded like he thought she was a blockhead after all, and he didn't. It sounded like he was saying she wasn't pretty, and what woman wanted to hear that?

He stared at her, wishing he could say what he felt. That she might be plain, but she was decent. That maybe she didn't have looks that would stop traffic, but she had integrity.

But he knew he was only going to make it worse if he said one more word about the way she looked or didn't look.

So he said, ''Holly, you're the best damn secretary a man could ever have.''

''You're not so bad as a boss either,'' she said, her tone light. But he knew from the way she looked at her screen and wouldn't look back at him that he'd handled it all wrong.

The problem was he knew all about women—and nothing about a woman like Holly. He retreated into his office, which he thought was a not bad form of damage control.

And he vowed he was staying there until next Saturday night when he was taking her to that dance, and then they were getting back to normal.

Or as normal as it could get without the kids here.

When she opened the door of her cottage the following Saturday, Blake stared at her, and knew it was never going to be normal again.

She stood in the doorway, the soft light from a lamp glowing over her shoulder, touching the side of her cheek, turning her hair to molten gold.

Her hair was down, and her glasses were gone. Her eyes looked huge and soft. Her cheekbones looked like something from *Vogue,* high, chiseled, proud. Her lips—

He found himself looking away from her lips in one hell of a hurry.

"Come in for a sec," she said. "I'm not quite ready. Can I get you a drink?"

He stumbled in the door behind her. She was wearing a soft beige shirt, embroidered horses galloping across the tops of her breasts, an even more dangerous area to look than her lips.

The shirt was tucked in to a waistband, cinched in by a tooled leather belt. He realized he could span her waist with his two hands. The ensemble was completed with a chocolate brown suede skirt that ended just below her knees, but its fullness contrasted delightfully with the slimness of her calves, the daintiness of her ankles.

Where had she been hiding this figure? Those suits she wore to the office made her look like a box.

And where had this face come from? He realized the glasses she normally wore were far too large, and had covered everything from her brow to mid-cheek. The glasses had hidden the curve of that cheekbone, the pert line of her nose; they had diminished the astonishing color and depth of her hazel eyes.

"Is something wrong?" she said uneasily. He saw the Holly he knew in the insecurity that flared in her eyes. "It was a barn dance, right? Western theme?"

A reminder he had not really gotten into the spirit of it. Jeans and a sports shirt. He hadn't even dug his cowboy boots out of the closet, mostly because they were real cowboy boots crusted with all that stuff real cowboys worked in and it would have taken him an hour to get them clean.

He smiled with what he hoped was reassurance. "Everything's fine."

He'd failed to reassure her, because she gave him an uncertain look. "Did you want a drink?"

"No thanks. I'll just wait."

She disappeared into a room at the back. Before she closed the door he caught a glimpse of a white lace bedspread that made his mouth go dry. It was so sensual and virginal at the same time.

What was he doing here? In his secretary's house? He looked around, trying to clear his mind of the new Holly.

Her house was the old Holly. Friendly and warm. She had a red-checked tablecloth on her small table that matched her curtains. A jar full of wildflowers sat in the center of it. She had some comfy-looking furniture grouped around the fireplace, her cat snoozing on the chair he might have chosen if he felt like sitting down.

Which he didn't. He felt edgy and ill at ease.

He wandered around. Some of the kids' pictures had made it into better frames and were hanging in here.

What was wrong with him? Why did he want to bolt for the door? Because she'd transformed from a guppie to a goldfish to an angel fish before he had time to adjust to it?

She came out of the bedroom. She had brown high-heeled cowboy boots on, and they made her look as tall and willowy as a model, an illusion that was dispelled when she did a self-conscious swirl for him.

His eyes widened as that dress lifted and showed legs
so long and shapely they could have belonged to a
chorus girl.

"Too much?" she asked him worriedly.

Way too much, but he gulped and mutely shook
his head. He held open the door to her cabin for her,
waited while she locked it, held open the door to the
ranch vehicle.

She slid in, put her hands primly in her lap and
looked straight ahead.

He got in and ordered himself to say something.
Anything.

But that was where the problem lay. What were the
rules here? Did he treat her the way he'd always
treated the women he dated? Did he instigate the light
banter with the slight overtones that promised a wild
romp later?

His tongue was as tied as a schoolboy's.

This was Holly.

He couldn't bring her that part of himself, the part
who only cared about getting his own needs met, and
to hell with everyone else.

"Uh, did you ever manage to get in touch with
Jamie Lynn's grandmother?"

"Yes. But nobody warned me she couldn't speak
English. And my high-school Spanish is dreadful. She
probably thinks her granddaughter has been mauled
by a bear or something."

They talked about that until it was pretty much exhausted. Ten or twenty seconds used up.

And then about the progress in the case, which took
another ten seconds, since progress seemed to have

ground to a halt, though Blake thought Rafe had looked grim last time he had spoken to him.

"I know who it is," he'd said. "I just can't prove it yet."

"Just give me the name," Blake had suggested silkily.

"As if," Rafe had said and managed to smile, and despite the professional frustrations he was feeling right now, his contentment in his new relationship with Libby Corbett had been in his eyes and his smile.

The rest of the trip to the Coltons' was uncomfortably silent.

When they arrived, the place was already packed. The barn had been opened and cleaned. Bales of straw and hay were stacked here and there for atmosphere, old saddles and harnesses were thrown over stall dividers.

Blake almost felt like when he walked in the whole room froze and every man was looking at her. He wanted to put his arm around her possessively. He wanted to shout to the world she was his.

Which was insane.

She was the secretary. His secretary. That was all.

At first he didn't recognize the boy coming through the crowd toward them, his face alight on Holly's. His hair had been cut, and his face shone with cleanliness and there was a light on in his eyes.

He stopped in front of them. "Do you remember me?" he demanded of Holly.

Blake thought it made you pretty unforgettable to hold a knife at someone.

"Of course I remember you, Tomas," Holly said,

as if the knife was the last thing she even associated with him. "How are you? How is Lucille?"

"Would you dance with me?" he asked with painful shyness.

"Of course I will," she said. "Thank you for asking."

She didn't even consult with her escort to see if that was okay with him.

He swore at himself. The kids came first. He knew that. Hadn't he showed her that? Why was he so annoyed? Wouldn't it have just made getting everything back to normal that much harder if he danced with her?

But he'd invited her to a dance. He supposed he was going to have to dance with her sometime.

Feeling grouchy and out of sorts, he repaired to the bar, debated a double rye and Coke, but settled for his customary Coke. With a sigh, he turned back to the dance floor.

The dance was a slow one, but thankfully Tomas was dancing with a certain stiff formality. Blake could have inserted a refrigerator between him and Holly.

She surprised him, though. She moved with a certain unselfconscious grace that he wouldn't have expected. Of course, that was back when he'd mistakenly thought he knew what to expect from Holly.

"My, my," Rafe said in his ear. "Who was that you came in with? Nobody I've seen around here before."

"You are no longer supposed to be looking," Blake reminded him tightly.

"I'm not looking for *me*," Rafe said indignantly. "I'm looking for *you*. You cannot believe how different life seems when you love someone. You just cannot believe it.''

''Whatever.''

''So who is she?''

''My secretary. Holly Lamb.''

Rafe stared at her in disbelief. ''My God,'' he finally said. ''It is her. What on earth happened?''

''Good question,'' Blake said, without any of his friend's enthusiasm.

''She's beautiful.''

''So it would seem.''

''You say that like it's a bad thing,'' Rafe said, giving him an incredulous look.

''It's a distraction that's not needed at the office.''

Rafe's look became stern. ''You know, Blake, you can take the Dudley-Do-Right thing too far. There are some things about the way you used to be that I miss.''

''Like what?'' Blake snapped.

''You used to be the kind of guy who said yes when the universe handed you a surprise package, an adventure.''

''That landed me in a lot of hard places, Rafe.''

''At least you were fun.''

''So, what are you saying?''

''Go dance with your girl.''

''She's not my girl. She's my secretary.''

''You brought her to a dance. I assume not to take shorthand. Go dance with her.''

But the first dance had ended, and another boy from the ranch was lined up right behind Tomas to dance with her. For a second it looked like a fight might erupt, before Holly intervened, putting her hand on

Tomas's shoulder and saying something that made him beam.

Seconds later Tomas was dancing with his little sister in his arms, and Holly was dancing with Brad Carmichael, who at age fifteen was a B & E artist of some note. The music was faster this time, and Blake nearly choked on his soda.

God, she was sexy. She moved her body with a grace and freedom nothing she had done in his office could have prepared him for.

Rafe, giving him one last annoyed look, went and got Libby.

The second song faded into a third. He had nearly built up his nerve to go over there, when he saw the new banker moving toward her. No bow tie tonight. The guy looked ridiculously handsome in jeans and a western shirt, a felt hat and boots.

How was she going to know he was a nerd when he was disguised like that?

Blake's drink was already empty. He went to the bar and got another. When he turned back the music had stopped, and there was a cluster of men, young and old, around his secretary.

He sighed and prepared himself for the longest night of his life.

Seven

"Holy, Holly," her best friend Jennifer O'Riley said, pushing through the crowded barn and swirling people, "I hardly recognized you."

"Oh for heaven's sake," Holly said, irritated. "I took off my glasses."

Jennifer, a beauty with flaming red hair and slanting green eyes, was looking at her less glamorous friend closely. "No, it's more than that."

"Okay," Holly offered grudgingly. "I put on a bit of makeup and did something a little different with my hair."

Jennifer was still looking at her intently, trying to solve some mystery.

"All right. I bought a new outfit!" Holly admitted.

"It's something else," Jennifer decided. "There's a certain glow about you. You look like a woman—"

Thankfully, Steve Darce, the new young bank manager was back asking Holly if she wanted to dance with him again. Because it gave Jenn no opportunity to finish what she was going to say, Holly said yes.

As if Holly didn't know exactly what Jenn planned to say. She had never been able to keep anything from her best friend. Jenn had seen the secret in her eyes.

She had seen it herself when she had looked in the mirror tonight. A certain light in her face that no makeup could give. A dreamy, faraway look in her eyes that had nothing to do with lashes so thick with mascara it felt like she was dripping soot.

Holly Lamb looked like a woman in love. And that, as much as the makeup and the outfit, was what was attracting all this attention.

Embarrassing attention. But a bit heady, too.

There was only one problem.

She looked over at Blake. He had not moved from the bar all night, though the bevy of beautiful women came and went. She recognized many of them. They dropped by the office, casually, as if they were just passing by. Since the Hopechest was ten miles from the nearest anything, it was pretty hard to just be in the neighborhood.

Torey Canfield, stewardess and part-time model. Rosemary Hansen, divorced, rich, gorgeous. Kaye McMurphy, counted on to make that stunning first impression when people first walked through the impressive glass-and-steel front doors of Springer. They fluttered around him, gorgeous perfect women, younger versions of her mother. There was one in particular tonight, Holly didn't know her name. Her hair was a cloud of gold around her head, and she had ignored the fact it was a barn dance and was dressed in a sequined form-fitting black sheath with a scoop neck. Even from a distance it was obvious. No underwear.

And even though she looked good tonight, Holly had no illusions. She would never look like that. She knew part of what made her so attractive tonight to all these men, young and old, was that she looked attainable. The nice, pleasant wholesome girl next door.

Not at all like the sophisticated woman in black who clung to the seat next to Blake.

Thoroughbred to her workhorse.

And Blake was a thoroughbred, too. Even the expression on his face—remote, glowering—seemed to add to his handsomeness not detract from it.

She recalled hearing that once. That a workhorse and a thoroughbred could not share the same harness.

And that probably said all that needed to be said about her and her boss. They were not in the same league. He had not noticed her when she had dressed out of the secretary's handbook, and he had not seemed to notice her duckling-to-swan metamorphosis tonight. He simply was not going to like her in the way she wanted to be liked by him, no matter what she did.

Not one comment on her appearance, the changes she had made.

Not one invitation to dance. No, it didn't take the sting out of it that he had not danced with anyone else either.

No, it didn't take the sting out of it when his friend Rory Sinclair went by with Peggy Honeywell and said to Holly in an undertone, "He never dances. Not even in college."

All that had done was make Holly feel ridiculously transparent, as if everyone in the whole world knew her secret and could see she was pining away for a man who did not see her the way she wanted to be seen.

It seemed to her romance was in the air tonight. In defiance of the tragedy that had ruled all their lives over the past few months, love grew, sweet and strong.

Rory Sinclair and Peggy Honeywell. Michael Longstreet and his wife, Suzanne. Now Rafe and Libby.

They were all here tonight, and Holly found herself resenting their obvious happiness. How easy it was, when she looked at these couples, to see how well suited they were, how they looked like they belonged together.

And little plain-Jane Holly Lamb was never going to look like that with her drop-dead gorgeous boss. Never.

"Hey," her dance partner, Steve Darce, said, "don't look sad. You'll give me a complex."

She forced herself to smile, and said lightly, "Well, that wouldn't do."

"I'd like to get to know you better. Where I don't have to yell over music. I heard there's a new restaurant open. The Red Herring. It's supposed to be pretty good. Do you want to check it out for dinner sometime?"

She kept her smile pasted on. "Let me think about it." Why? Why think about it? She needed to get on with her life, quit wishing for things that weren't going to happen.

Steve was a nice guy. All right, he didn't have Blake's commanding presence. Or Blake's penetrating gray eyes. Or Blake's beautiful silky full hair. He also didn't have a dozen gorgeous women hovering around him all night.

He had nice plain, clean-cut features, thinning reddish hair, an earnest way and a good sense of humor.

Why not go to the Red Herring with him?

It would be too pathetic if she just spent her whole life waiting for the thing that was never going to happen.

"Sure," she said. "Let's go for dinner."

He beamed at her. "I'll pick you up tomorrow night around six."

She wanted to protest that was much too soon. Two nights out in a row? But she knew wanting to put off her date with Steve was just part of keeping an unreasonable hope alive.

"That would be fine," she said. The dance ended, and suddenly Jenn was beside her.

"Last dance," Jenn hissed in her ear. "For God's sake, go ask him."

"Who?" Holly said primly.

Jenn rolled her eyes. "Go. For once in your life do something daring."

Holly thought that was particularly unfair. She had been daring. Couldn't Jenn see that? The hair, the makeup, the clothes. It had all felt pretty daring, until she had seen that number in the black sequins. Now she felt like little Miss Goody-Two-Shoes.

But maybe Jenn was right. She had to take one

more chance. She had to roll all the dice before she tossed in the towel for good.

Aching with trepidation, she crossed the dance floor. Just as she pushed through the throng milling around the bar, she saw the woman in black pulling at his arm, obviously making the very same request she had come to make. She turned away.

"Holly!"

She turned back. Blake was coming toward her, the woman in black perching on her seat with a pout that turned menacing when she saw Holly.

"Would you dance with me?"

Her mouth fell open. She blinked. She glanced at the woman in black and back at him. She had been chosen over that? Maybe miracles did happen.

"I don't dance very well," he said leaning toward her, "or very often. But I did bring you."

Oh. Nice of him to notice. The obligatory dance. Still, she could not refuse.

She allowed him to take her elbow and guide her onto the crowded dance floor. The music began. Fate having a snicker at her. One of her favorite songs of all time, so sweetly romantic, so full of hope and promise.

As the song's opening bars played, his one hand took hers, the other nestled in the hollow of her hip.

When all else has failed me,
When I'm weary and torn,
Love whispers to me,
And my spirit is reborn.

Holly closed her eyes and let the soaring vocals of Annie Adams pick her up, soothe her. The scent of

him filled her senses, his hand in hers made anything
seem possible.

Oh, I've walked alone
All the days of my life,
But love promises me
An end to heartache and strife.

He was a terrible dancer, and it didn't matter to her
one little bit. But then, as if he confessed that to himself, he gave up the pretense of dancing. His hand
moved to the small of her back and he tugged her
gently into the wall of his chest, and swayed against
her.

Like the sailor who comes home from the sea,
The warrior home from the dying;
Bring your broken wings to me.
Love mends those hearts that are crying.

Holly had known that this place existed somewhere
on this earth for her. She had always known. That
one day she would feel this. Safe. Protected. Cher-
ished. Loved.

She was ridiculous to feel those things.

It was only a dance. Yet, she could feel the simple
strength in him, in his hand against her back, in the
heart that beat so steadily under the soft caress of her
cheek against his chest.

Her bones were melting. If she had no other moment, it felt like this one would be enough to sustain
her all the days of her life, to fix her broken wings

and mend her heart, to make anything that was wrong with her world right.

The music stopped, and yet still he held her to him. And when she dared look up into his face, he was looking down at her with faint puzzlement, as if he had never seen her before, as if he had never felt what he had just felt.

As though he only suddenly realized the music had stopped, he stepped away from her. His hands remained at her hips for a precious moment longer, before he let them drop to his sides, then looked away from her and ran a hand through his hair.

"Shall we go?" he said.

She nodded, and looped her arm through the arm he offered her, but she knew, with a sinking feeling, that her moment was over.

But Jenn didn't seem to think so. She was grinning wickedly. "I'll call you tomorrow."

Jenn assumed Holly knew what to do next. When she didn't. Should she suggest they go for a drink? Did she invite him in? Did she kiss him if he came in?

The thought of kissing him actually made her feel weak with wanting.

"You seemed to have a good time tonight," he said in the vehicle.

"It was fun," she said.

"After all you've done at Hopechest you deserved a fun night."

She glanced at him quickly, because that didn't seem to be said with the least bit of sincerity. He actually seemed very remote, as if she had annoyed him by having fun.

"You didn't seem to enjoy yourself."

He shrugged. "Two left feet."

"Not that I noticed," she said softly.

All too soon, before she had a chance to work up her nerve to ask him if he wanted to go somewhere for a drink, he had pulled the ranch vehicle into its parking stall in front of the office and walked her across the street.

The moonlight made it a perfect night for romance. The stars winked at them from the heavens.

A fact he didn't seem to notice. He seemed distant, and faraway. He didn't touch her and he certainly didn't attempt to kiss her. "Good night, Holly," he said softly, then turned and was gone.

Disappointed, she went in the door and closed it behind her. She went into the bathroom and looked at her face in the mirror It was still there—that look of a woman in love. But there was something else there now, too. A certain sadness that made her eyes look huge and lonesome.

She tugged off the skirt and shirt and slipped into her beautiful old-fashioned nightdress. It was pure white, high-collared, embroidered down the front.

In the darkness of her cabin, she went and stood at her window, watched the light go on in his apartment. For a moment, her breath caught in her throat, she watched his silhouette as he took off his clothes.

Her heart hammered in her throat.

A bolder woman, that woman in black, would have crossed the street.

Instead Holly turned away. She might not be a bolder woman, like her mother, but she realized she was not the dowdy secretary she had been portraying for eight months either. He had said to her she was the rarest of things. A person who knew how to be herself.

And she felt she needed to live up to that.

Herself was the girl who looked back at her from the mirror moments ago. Not trying to look professional, not hiding behind her glasses. A disguise was a disguise. Hiding her true assets was as much a lie as her mother's paint and dye.

Not the most beautiful girl, but not ugly either.

With a sigh, she went into the kitchen and pulled a sack of black plastic garbage bags out of the kitchen drawer. She went into her bedroom and opened the closet door. Without one bit of regret she slid the suits from their hangers, the black one, the gray one, the navy one, the white linen that she had been saving for summer. She dropped them into the bag. Tomorrow she would take them to Goodwill, and see if she could talk Jenn into a quick shopping trip with her.

Jennifer, of course, was thrilled to be asked to go shopping.

And Holly, rather than feeling a heaviness of heart, felt a wonderful excitement as they picked items that suited her and the casual atmosphere of the ranch office. It felt like she was uncovering herself, discovering herself.

"This one," Jenn said, holding up a green silk shirt. "With these jeans."

Holly looked at the price of the shirt and shook her head.

"Holly, what are you spending your money on? You have no expenses. No rent. No children. You drive a thirteen-year-old car that should have been taken off the road six years ago.''

Holly thought of the butterscotch candies, and the goldfish and the picture frames. She bought teddy bears, too, because sometimes the little ones were so frightened when they came, and sometimes they had never had a single toy to call their own, so she kept a selection of beautiful brand-new bears to give them. It hadn't taken her long to discover the older children needed those teddy bears just as much as the younger ones.

Still, it was her turn. She took the green shirt and pressed the soft fabric to her face.

Jenn twirled her around, so that she faced the mirror. ''Look,'' she said softly.

Holly gasped. With that shade of green her eyes looked as luminous and as lovely as emeralds.

By the end of the day, her arms were loaded with parcels. Jenn insisted she buy only what she loved. Nothing she felt mediocre about was allowed.

She invited Jenn back to her place for a quick cup of tea before she had to get ready to go for dinner with Steve Darce.

Jenn helped her pick an outfit to wear, and they giggled like schoolgirls as she put it on. The green shirt and white linen pants, a new pair of green earrings that intensified the illusion that her eyes were emeralds.

Holly had turned to get the boiling water when Jenn asked her, ''So, does Blake have a clue what you feel?''

She kept her back deliberately turned, poured boiling water into the kettle, tossed in a tea bag. "Blake?"

"You know," Jenn said, "your boss?"

"How I feel about what?" Holly asked. She took a deep breath, set the tea things on a tray and turned with a bright smile to her friend.

"About him."

The smile crumpled, and the tea things slid to one end of the tray. She set them on the table with a bang and sank down into her chair.

"And what do you think I feel about him?" she asked. She poured the tea. Her hand was trembling.

"I think you're madly in love with him."

Holly spilled some tea and set down the pot. "What makes you think that?" she said.

"I saw the look on your face last night. I saw you dancing with him."

"Oh, God." Holly moaned and gave up all pretense of pouring the tea. "I'm obvious. How pathetic."

"I don't think it's pathetic," Jenn said. "I think it's wonderful."

"Wonderful? Are you crazy? Did you see the women around him last night? How gorgeous and glamorous they all were?"

"I did notice that. I also noticed he didn't seem to pay the least bit of attention to them. Every time I looked at him, he was glaring at you."

"Oh, sure. With Torey Canfield and Rosemary Hansen hanging all over him. Not to mention that vision in black."

"I know what I saw," Jenn said stubbornly. "He was looking at you. And you were the one he danced with. Besides, Torey and Rosemary and Kaye have been flirting with him for years. I haven't noticed them getting anywhere.''

Come to think of it, when they visited him in the office, Holly could not remember him ever seeming too impressed. Polite. Yes. Smitten? Flattered?

No.

She felt this little flag of hope unfurling in her chest. Could it be she might be the one for him, after all?

"You're going to absolutely hate what I tell you next," Jenn said, finishing pouring the tea and handing her a cup.

Holly was scared to ask.

"You need to let him know how you're feeling."

Holly set down the cup. "What?"

"I knew it. You're just the picture of the perfect secretary when you're around him, aren't you? Little Miss Efficient. Competent. Professional."

"I hope you're not suggesting I shouldn't be those things," Holly said huffily.

"Not at all. But you can be those things and let him know how you're feeling."

"I cannot. What would you have me say? 'I've finished typing this letter. P.S. I love you'?"

"I didn't say *tell* him, I said let him know. Show him."

"I wouldn't have a clue how to do that," Holly said.

"That's what I thought. You're working so hard at keeping your feelings in. Just let them out. Put flowers on his desk. Bake him cookies. Quit trying to hide all the warmth you feel for him.''

"I can't," Holly said.

"Why on earth not?"

"I'm scared," she whispered. "I've never felt this way before. I'm terrified."

"Of course you're terrified," Jenn said calmly. "And it's okay to be terrified. It's just not okay to be ruled by it."

There was a knock on the door.

Holly's eyes flew to the clock. "That's Steve already. What do you think? Should I tell him I can't go?"

Jenn shook her head indulgently. "You don't know the first thing about playing this game, do you? No, you go for dinner with the delightful Mr. Darce tonight. I bet Blake is watching out his window right now."

"He is not."

"And tomorrow you don't say a single word about it. Now go and answer the door. And if you can find it in yourself, give Steve a little kiss on the cheek in way of greeting."

Holly went to the door and opened it.

But somehow she couldn't find that in herself.

Eight

Blake looked glumly out his window. He should have been happy to see activity on the ranch again, but it was the wrong kind of activity. That little cabin across the street had become like Grand Central Station all of a sudden.

An hour ago, after disappearing early this morning, Holly had pulled up in her little silver rust-covered car.

Her friend had been right behind her in the fire-engine-red Camaro that clashed with her hair.

Her friend was good-looking in that Torey Canfield way. Glamorous. Well-dressed. Polished.

Empty.

Loaded down with parcels, the two women had disappeared inside the cabin.

Now another car had pulled up in front of her

place. Conservative. A white New Yorker, obviously new. Blake told himself he must have something better to do than spy on his secretary.

But he stayed at the window.

The banker got out. The one who had monopolized her all of last night. He still wasn't wearing the little bow tie that would have clued Holly in that he was a nerd.

No, today he looked like the captain of the football team in his Dockers, sports shirt and a black leather jacket.

Black leather jackets, Blake strongly felt, were the exclusive domain of people who rode motorcycles. He hated it when that line was crossed.

What was the banker doing here? He hoped he'd come to get her friend.

But it was Holly who came to the door. For a moment she leaned toward the banker, and Blake had the hopeless feeling she was going to kiss him.

But then she didn't. She ducked back in the house. Hopefully to call her friend. But her friend did not come out.

She did, carrying a sweater.

She was wearing something he had never seen her wear before. A green blouse that hugged her slender body like a glove, casual slacks. He bet that blouse would make her eyes green as emeralds.

The banker held open the door of his car for her, and she smiled and slid in.

Blake watched as they drove away, and then looked back at her porch. Her friend Jenn was out there now, looking straight at his window.

She was grinning wickedly, as if she had caught

him spying. With a jaunty wave, she climbed in her own car and was gone.

Annoyed, he dropped the shade and turned away. He spent the rest of the evening pretending to work, and listening for a car to pull up in front of her place.

At around ten the sound he had been waiting for came. Don't look, he ordered himself.

A thought hit him that turned his blood to ice.

What if the banker went in? And didn't come back out?

Fallon, he told himself firmly, it's none of your business. Besides, Holly wasn't that kind of girl. Or at least a week ago she hadn't been. He didn't like the feeling that he didn't know who Holly was anymore. It felt like some great loss. The worst kind of loss, that kind where you hadn't appreciated what you had until it was gone.

He was walking toward his window. He couldn't believe this! He had strictly ordered his mind to sit down and shut up. But his mind, acting like a practiced secret agent who had turned off his bedroom light so he couldn't be seen spying, took him to the window and pulled back the shade a bit.

Holly and the banker were on her porch. His car was still running, which Blake took to be a good sign. The banker knew he wasn't staying. He was also on the bottom step, and Holly was on the top one. Blake also took that as a good sign, as the physical distance between the pair did not bode well if the date was thinking of claiming a kiss. Unless he excelled at hurdles. Thankfully he didn't look like the athletic type. Or the type to boldly steal a kiss.

Even so, Blake felt something shift inside him at

the very thought of someone else kissing her. It was like his blood turned from ice to fire, as if he went into a fiercely instinctive mode, like a male grizzly determined to protect his territory.

He dropped the shade and took a step back, contemplating this violent reaction to the thought of Holly kissing someone else.

She wasn't his woman. She was his secretary.

Blake realized, with shock, how badly he wanted to kiss her. To taste her lips with his own, to feel the curves of her pressed eagerly against him as she had been when they danced that last dance together last night.

He went back to his lonely table and sat down, stunned, like a man who had been too close when a bomb had gone off.

He wanted to kiss his secretary. And he wanted it badly. And not only that, he also wanted to punch the daylights out of that guy down there who looked like he might beat him to it.

Even in his debilitated state he was aware when the car left, aware of something within him sighing with relief.

He shook his head, trying to regain his senses. He was her boss. And that made everything he was contemplating wrong. Plain and simple. Wrong. He was a professional man, known for his work ethic and his integrity. Where did wooing one's secretary fit into that equation?

Plain and simple? It didn't.

Especially in light of his position here. These kids needed to be around people who always did the honorable thing. Always.

The kids aren't even here, the side of him that once stole motorcycles told him with fiendish waggling of eyebrows. That part of him would be down his steps and across the road and on her doorstep before the banker cleared the main gate. That part of him would sweep her into his arms, coax out her wild side—

This is Holly, he reminded his darker twin impatiently. Holly was not the kind of girl you had a quick tumble with and then walked away from. He wasn't prepared to lose the best secretary he'd ever had over a moment of wildness, a momentary loss of control.

Blake Fallon was a big advocate of self-control. It was practically the motto by which he ran the ranch. He was also a big advocate of practice what you preach.

He couldn't just pretend to have integrity, he had to have it all the time. Even when no one was looking. These kids in particular had never had good examples set for them. Many of them had parents on the other side of the law, parents with addiction problems, parents who could rationalize anything to get what they wanted.

Blake felt it was crucial his behavior be exemplary in every area. He knew that feeling had intensified since his own father had taken a gun and tried to murder Joe Colton at his own birthday party.

Rafe had implied last night at the dance Blake was overdoing it. That he had become rigid and wasn't even fun anymore.

And he supposed that was true. Somewhere along the line, in his transformation from wild street kid, to responsible, respected adult, he had lost something— the boy who laughed with such reckless abandon, who took delight in scorning the "shoulds," who took chances, and who was fearless in accepting whatever opportunity life presented him with.

Holly wouldn't have liked that boy.

Annoyed with himself that everything came back to her, he stripped off his shirt and jeans, slid into bed and begged for sleep.

Instead, he thought of Holly, her arms around Tomas, the tender look in her eyes as she had caught Blake's gaze over the top of Tomas's head.

And he knew Holly would have liked the wild boy he used to be very, very much. Good girls were always intrigued with wild boys.

Dawn was breaking before he finally fell asleep. And so he did something he had never done before. He slept in. He was late for work.

Holly was already at her desk when he came through the front door.

He had hoped the glasses and hair would be back in place, and that she would be back in one of those formidable outfits that made her look so straight-lined—about as sexy as a ruler.

But when he came through the door the first thing he noticed was that her hair was still down, flowing in a shining river down to her shoulders. He wished he would have touched it at the dance, when he had the opportunity.

The glasses were still missing.

And gone was the suit that looked like it had been mail-ordered from the Miss Manners Office Collection.

She was wearing a soft white V-necked sweater that hugged her slender form. He thought that fabric was called angora. It was a material that begged to be touched.

His mouth went dry, and he ordered himself to be a man of complete and uncompromising integrity.

"Good morning, Blake."

Had she always had a voice like that? Like music? Like bells tinkling?

"Holly." He heard the curtness in his tone and saw her flinch slightly from it. He closed the office door and walked by her, but he made the mistake of sliding one more look at her out the corner of his eye.

Without the glasses her eyes were more expressive than ever.

And she didn't just look hurt by his cool greeting, she looked exhausted.

Integrity, be damned.

"Are you all right?" he asked her, looking more closely. "You don't look good." The look of hurt in her eyes deepened, and he wished he could pull the words back into his mouth, because she had really never looked better. He clarified. "You look tired."

Too late he considered her weariness might be from mooning over the young banker. He certainly didn't want to invite her confidence about that.

"Oh," she said, getting up and going to the filing cabinet, "I'm not sleeping well."

He stared at her skirt. Navy blue. Tight. Short. Her legs were long and slender and perfectly shaped.

The new Holly was a serious danger to his ethics. But it was the old Holly he saw in her eyes and heard in her voice, and it was the old Holly he could not walk away from as if he was not concerned, as if she was just a function and not a human being.

A human being he had come to like and respect very much.

"How come?" he asked softly.

She turned and gave him a wan smile. "I've been having bad dreams."

"About?"

"I keep dreaming about the water being poisoned." She closed her eyes, pressed a hand to her forehead.

He could not stop himself. He went to her, put his hand on her shoulder, turned her to him. "Tell me about them."

The sweater felt like nothing he had ever felt before. The softness, especially with her skin below it, so sensual he had a sudden wild fantasy of picking her up, tossing her on that sofa, kissing her until she was breathless, until that weariness was chased from her eyes, replaced with something quite different.

He dropped his hand from her shoulder as if he'd been burned. So much for Mr. Self-Control Fallon.

"I'm just being silly. It doesn't matter. I mean they're only dreams."

"Tell me about them," he said again.

She hesitated, then looked over his shoulder. "At first it was a monster. Huge and shapeless, red eyes and foul saliva dropping from his mouth. It was an old-fashioned well, like a wishing well, and he'd pour stuff in it. Luminous green and boiling."

"And then?"

She shuddered. "The monster kept changing forms in my dreams. And so did the substance he was pouring in the well. Sometimes it's like tar and other times it's full of horrible things."

''What does the monster change into?''

''Last night,'' she whispered, ''he turned into a man. I had the most dreadful feeling he was someone I know.''

Blake registered that and knew the truth in it. Every man had a monster within him. A part of him that would cross the line between what was right and wrong because he could talk himself into it.

For instance, right now it would be so easy to brush aside the ''hands-off'' vow he had made about his secretary and gather her to him, run his hand down the silk of her hair, feel her breath against his chest.

But what was his *real* motive? To comfort her? Or to satisfy the part of himself that wanted to know all of her, solve her mysteries, taste her lips?

He settled for giving her shoulder a fraternal little pat. ''You can always call me if you're frightened in the night.''

The words were out before he had given them proper thought. He was barreling toward the danger zone. Going to her in the night? He bet she wore one of those long white nightgowns, like the ones they wore in *Little House on the Prairie*. He thought of being her comfort and strength in the night.

He was aware she was looking at him, something glowing in her eyes he had not seen before.

Probably because of the glasses, he told himself firmly.

''Thanks, Blake. I won't need to call you. It's good enough knowing you're so close.''

If she had said that last week—with her hair put up primly, and in her conservative suit, her glasses swallowing up half her face—it wouldn't have meant what it meant right now.

It wouldn't have set his heart to racing, made his face feel like it was on fire.

Without one more word, he escaped into his office. But his escape was thwarted somewhat.

She had put a bouquet of flowers on his desk. Wildflowers. He saw them growing around the ranch all the time.

His office was an austere space, much like his apartment above it. It contained a metal desk, nothing fancy, bookshelves, file cases, a couple of chairs. The floor was tiled, and the windows had metal Venetians on them, no curtains.

Everything was in its place.

Those flowers were like an invasion, of something softer and warmer and more colorful. It was like she had found a way to be in his office without even being here.

Which would only make his vow harder to keep.

He picked up the vase, firmly, before he could change his mind. He took them out to her office, set them on the corner of her desk.

"I'm allergic," he said.

For a second he contemplated that. A man who had taken a vow of complete integrity telling such an innocuous lie.

He tried to slip back into his office before the look in her eyes registered, but he was not successful.

Hurt.

He had hurt her.

And somehow he couldn't convince himself that was what integrity was about.

By the end of the week he thought he was going out of his mind. He wondered if he could order her back into those dowdy gray and navy suits that had made it so easy to see her only as a part of his office.

Not furniture, exactly, but just a part of the infrastructure that kept everything running smoothly and efficiently. A background item that was easy to ignore.

Now she was in the foreground, in a new wardrobe that was incredibly flattering to her, that made her not his secretary, but a woman. The old clothes, it seemed to him, had successfully hidden the parts of her that were most dangerous to him.

Her passion. Had the banker brought out this side in her? The new look seemed to coincide with the banker's interest. Blake was desperate to know, and yet he could not bring himself to ask.

If she detected his interest, she might reciprocate it. Then what? Worse, she might not. Then what?

Nothing seemed smooth anymore. Efficient, yes, but not smooth.

He couldn't ask her to write a letter for him without noticing her. The silky shine of her hair. The color of her eyes. The delicate line of her leg when she crossed them in those short skirts, and took dictation.

Calling her into his office, asking her for a file, everything had become about battling the monster within him.

He noticed she looked tired some mornings, and longed to ask if the dreams troubled her, but did not know where his longing would lead. To her bed? Where he could protect her and hold her if she cried in the night?

To her bed. There was the truth of it. The bottom line. He had become sexually attracted to his secretary. Longed to know if that passive exterior hid the passionate interior the new wardrobe suggested.

Longed, if he was brutally honest, to have her give that part of herself to just him.

"I'm losing my mind," he muttered.

"Pardon, Blake?"

"Don't sneak up on me," he snapped.

"Sneak up on you?" she said, astounded and hurt. "I knocked on the door."

He knew he was being a complete jerk with her. Acting as if it was her fault he was going through this, trying to build a high wall so that she couldn't climb it.

"And something else," he said, "don't bring me any more cookies."

Don't you know what you're doing to me? How hard you are making it to fight? Don't you know how I want to bury my head in your neck, allow your tenderness to touch me?

"I'm on a diet," he muttered.

"*You're* on a diet?" she said, incredulously.

"That's what I said."

"I think there's a name for that disorder. But I thought only girls got it."

Once he would have laughed. How he longed for those days when he used to laugh with her. "I don't want your damned cookies."

Even as her face became coolly chilly, and he saw her pull back her shoulders proudly, he registered far more clearly what she didn't want him to see. He saw her crumpling inside and despised himself.

"Holly, I'm sorry. You're not the only one having trouble sleeping at night." Though he could not use bad dreams as his excuse. He was lying awake contemplating the ethics of what he felt for his secretary.

He despised himself even more for how easily she forgave him.

"It's been an enormous strain on you," she said quietly. "I know you want the kids back here."

God, yes. A ranch full of kids yelling and running and jumping and needing things from him was just what he needed to fill up his mind, to remove from it the intensity of focus he now had on her.

"I do," he said. But he couldn't bring them back just to make his life easier, just as something to insert between him and her.

He longed for his life of a week ago, when everything had been so blessedly simple. He longed for how he used to be able to talk to her, for the laughter they had shared that seemed to have shriveled between them now. Not her fault, any of it, but he wanted to blame her, anyway.

"Why don't you go over to the Coltons and have lunch with the kids?" she suggested. "Bring the cookies."

"That's a good idea," he said, glancing at the clock. If he left right now, he'd be there right at lunchtime.

Don't ask her, he ordered himself. But his mind was like a crew in mutiny—it rarely listened to him anymore, flaunted his commands.

"So, you want to come along?"

Something leapt in her eyes, and then died. She turned away from him.

"No thanks," she said.

"Okay." Her reply hurt him, even though he should have expected nothing less. How had this happened? How had they gone from having such a good working relationship to this?

He sighed as she quietly closed the door behind her. He accepted full responsibility.

He shrugged into his jacket, and at the last minute, remembered her cookies.

They'd been there when he arrived this morning. A huge plate of cookies, dripping with chocolate chips and smelling of heaven.

He felt like he was battling the devil, struggling to be the man he had to be, temptation put in his path all the time.

Small temptations. Like cookies.

Cookies that would taste of dreams he had long since decided were for other men. Dreams of little houses that smelled of cookies baking and rang with the laughter of children playing.

What did a man like him know of such things?

What he knew was that dysfunction was multigenerational. He was the son of a man who had attempted murder. He was only a few steps removed from his own past.

He didn't know how to be part of a family. He didn't know how to be the man Holly would need for him to be.

It occurred to him that without his permission everything was escalating. He wasn't just thinking of ravishing her on the couch anymore.

No, his thoughts were far scarier than that now.

Little temptations paving the way.

Didn't she know if he ate one of these cookies, he might be lost? That the control he exercised was a fragile thing, and he did not know what would push him over the edge?

He shook his head in self-mockery. What kind of man thought his entire fate turned on a cookie?

Rebelliously, he took one and popped the whole thing in his mouth.

A mistake.

Ecstasy. One step closer to being lost.

Nine

"**I**t's backfiring," Holly said, opening the cardboard box of Chinese food that Jenn had brought for supper. She looked at the pork dumplings without interest, took one to be polite.

"What do you mean it's backfiring?" Jenn didn't have her lack of appetite at all. Her plate was already piled high with the Szechuan-style Chinese food they both preferred.

Holly pushed a grain of rice across her plate with her chopstick. "At least I used to feel like Blake liked me. I've wrecked what we had. He used to be friendly, now he's curt. He used to ask my opinions on things, now he avoids me. He used to be good-humored and fun and now he's stern and remote."

"Really?" Jenn asked avidly.

"Really," Holly said glumly. "I've ruined everything."

"My honest opinion is there was nothing to ruin. You loved him, he didn't know you were alive. I think you're reading this all wrong."

"In what way?"

"He knows you're alive."

"He hates me!"

"Hates you?" Jenn asked with interest. "What would make you say that?"

Holly told her about the cookies.

"My," Jenn said, putting a whole pork dumpling in her mouth and chewing thoughtfully, "doesn't that strike you as rather a strong reaction to cookies? What did he say exactly, again?"

"'I don't want your damned cookies.'"

Jenn's eyes went very wide. "This is better than I hoped."

"Oh, sure."

"Think about it, Holly. He doesn't want the damned cookies, he wants you!"

Holly took a desultory bite of her ginger beef and gave her friend a suspicious look. "Are you reading too many romance novels?" It was her friend who had introduced her to the delights of a good love story.

"There's no such thing as reading too many. I read two a week, three in a good week."

"Real life doesn't work like that!" Holly wailed.

"Holly, cynicism does not suit you. If you're going to get that man, you have to trust me and follow my instructions exactly."

Holly was not sure she wanted to turn her romantic life so completely into Jenn's keeping. Her friend had admirers coming out her ears, it was true, but her longest relationship had lasted just under six weeks.

"What are your instructions?" she asked reluctantly.

"More of everything. More cookies. More accidental meeting of hands. Turn up the heat. Bring a romantic picnic lunch packed for two."

"And if he says 'I don't want your damned lunch'?"

"Then you say 'Fine, I'll call Steve and he can come eat it with me.'"

To Holly it did sound like the plot of a romance novel. Lure the boss in with romantic gestures and if that didn't work, try to make him jealous. What Jenn didn't seem to get was that Blake had to care about her in order to be jealous.

"I don't know," she said uneasily. "I think I should just go back to the way I was before. Everything seemed so much more comfortable."

"Comfortable?" Jenn said. "Good grief. Is that what you want—comfortable?"

"Yes," Holly said firmly.

"Well, then stick with Steve. You'll get comfortabled near to death. You can take up golfing and learn to play cribbage. But if you want your heart to beat faster and your temperature to heat up and skyrockets to go off, Blake is your man."

Holly wanted to deny she wanted all those things. But she couldn't.

"So are you ready to instigate Plan B, for Week 2?"

"No," Holly said.

"Holly, it's one week out of your life. For heaven's sake, be bold, be daring."

"That's what you said last week."

"I tell you, it's working. You've got to be ready to fight for what you want, girl."

"You're not there in that office. He snapped at me about a misplaced file—and it turned out he had misplaced it!"

"You're crumpling his defenses. Don't take the pressure off now, he'll have a chance to rebuild, and they'll go up stronger than before. You know what? He's a control freak, and you're threatening his control. He probably has a rule book somewhere that says 'Thou shalt not romance your secretary.'"

Even Holly had to admit there might be a kernel of truth in that observation. "What exactly would you pack in a romantic picnic lunch?"

"Oh," Jenn said, thrilled to be asked, "white wine, croissants, two kinds of cheese and strawberries. Strawberries are the most romantic food."

"What do you want to bet he's allergic to them?" Holly said sourly.

"Promise me you'll try it. Promise."

Holly felt trapped.

"Say it."

"Okay. I'll try it."

"What day?"

"Jenn—"

"What day?"

"Does it have to be next week?"

"Yes."

"Friday, then."

"Good. That gives you four days to build up to it.

Lots of accidental nudges, long looks, nice gestures. More cookies. Those seemed to get a great reaction.''

''I'd hate to hear your definition of great,'' Holly said.

Still, there was a certain relief in having a plan, instead of just floundering along in a kind of desperate misery hoping she chanced upon the right thing.

She dressed carefully Monday morning. The white angora sweater seemed to get a reaction that she liked and he didn't. She thought the navy skirt was a little too short, but she hadn't missed him sneaking peeks at her legs.

She eyed herself in the mirror, her stomach in knots. She just wasn't suited for this kind of thing. She picked up her purse.

''Another day in the trenches,'' she told herself as she headed across the street, cookies in hand.

It occurred to her this war would be so much easier if there was no emotion involved, if she could play her part with detachment.

But as soon as he walked in, his hair still wet and curling from the shower, she felt totally flustered. Wordlessly, she handed him the bag of cookies.

He opened them, looked in and looked angry. Angry. That was the part Jenn didn't get to see.

''I thought I told you—''

''Oh, you did,'' she said, amazed by how composed she sounded. ''In no uncertain terms. Didn't want my damned cookies, I think you put it. I made them for the kids. You have a staff meeting at the Coltons' at eleven.'' And she went back to her typing.

But she noticed he stood there for a long time, staring at her before he moved on.

When he left for the meeting he didn't have the cookies with him. She found the bag on his desk, half devoured.

And for the first time in a long time, she found herself smiling. And then laughing. Jenn was right. He wasn't showing her how he was feeling with all that crankiness, he was hiding how he was feeling.

For the first time since she had started toying with this daisy of I-love-you, I-love-you-not, she had a feeling she might end up holding the I-love-you petal. It lit a light in her heart that he could not begin to put out.

She did everything Jenn had told her. She touched his arm when she talked to him, and noticed with pleasure rather than pain how swiftly he pulled away. That was not the reaction of a man who was feeling nothing. That was the reaction of a man who was feeling way too much.

Still, on Friday she was terrified as she hauled in her huge wicker basket and set it on the corner of her desk.

He stopped in the doorway as soon as he saw it.

"Someone sending you gifts?" he asked.

"No."

Did he really look relieved? Really?

"What's this about, then?" He came over and peeled back the checked cover.

"I brought it. I was hoping you'd have lunch with me today."

He flipped the cover back as if it had pricked him with thorns. "Holly, I can't. Not today. I—"

She smiled sweetly. "That's all right. I'll ask Steve. It would be a shame for that to go to waste."

"Who the hell is Steve? The banker, I suppose?"

"As a matter of fact, he is a banker. I wasn't aware that was a bad thing."

He glared at her. She was aware of holding her breath, but she would not look away from him. Was he going to call her bluff?

"Actually," he said, finally, "I think maybe we need to get out of the office. It seems tense in here lately."

"Does it?" she asked innocently.

"I know a great place for a picnic."

If she wasn't careful she would blow it all now by leaping up out of her chair and throwing herself into his arms.

Instead, she turned to her computer and said, "Great, I can't wait."

At noon he came out of his office and took the basket off her desk. "Are those shoes okay for a little hike?"

She nodded, and soon they were walking side by side along a well-worn trail that led off the ranch and up through the timber.

And amazingly, it was like everything was all right between them again. Blake laughed and helped her up the trail; they popped the cork on the wine halfway up, because they had forgotten water.

He took a swig and handed her the bottle. She didn't wipe it before she took a sip, too.

It was like they were old friends who had not talked for a long time. And when he took her hand to help her up the last little rocky stretch, it felt like that was where her hand was meant to be. In his, traveling the trails of life together.

They arrived on a little outcrop that overlooked the deserted ranch and the countryside around it. The view was panoramic and the sun was mellow and rich.

She spread the blanket that was at the bottom of the basket, and took out the picnic items. He stretched out on his side, propped up on his elbow.

"This was a great idea, Holly."

"Thanks. I thought so."

"Things haven't been the same between us for a while," he said softly, regarding her intently.

"Yes, I know."

"And why do you think that is?"

She shrugged. "I don't know." Jennifer had forgotten to coach her on this part.

"I don't know either," he said. "But I like this better."

"Me, too."

They talked about the ranch and the Coltons and the kids. He told her some ideas he was working on for a new ranch program for the boys in The Shack.

"They're the ones who are special to you, aren't they, Blake, those boys who have flirted with the dark side of life?"

"Those boys are me," he said.

"I know."

"Do you?"

"Yes." And she did. She knew him to his soul.

"How can you know all the things I've tried so hard to keep secret?" he asked.

"I know all about that wild guy in you, Blake, the one you've tried to tame and never quite succeeded."

His eyebrows shot up.

Suddenly she didn't need Jenn to tell her what to do. She knew. She just knew.

"I know," she said softly, "how much that wild boy has wanted to do this."

And just like that she kissed him. She leaned forward and touched his lips with hers.

He froze, and for a moment, just a moment, she thought she had overplayed her hand, that her instincts had failed her.

But then he groaned, a groan of defeat, and surrender and wanting.

And his hand trailed down her hair and found the back of her neck, and it pulled her in closer to him.

His lips were not tentative as hers were. She realized immediately that he did not share her innocence.

His lips were experienced, and they claimed hers totally, commanded her. Her mouth parted beneath that command, and his tongue found the warm hollow of her mouth.

She was shocked by how rapidly an innocent kiss could catch fire—and thrilled by the nameless sensations that shuddered through her as his passion deepened.

It felt like all her life she had waited for this one moment.

And for him to share it with her.

This was the place where dreams met reality, and where some dreams would have shattered under the force of the collision.

But that was not what happened to the dream of Holly Lamb.

It took wing. Her love for him took wing. Nothing in her held back from him. Nothing. She gave everything she was to that meeting of lips—her heart, her soul, her fire.

And it felt like he gave everything he was back to her.

In the kiss were all his secrets—a wild passion, a part of him that was untamed and uncontrolled. But it held also the essence of the man. His great will and integrity, his solidness.

What she had never known before was that a kiss was not an ending.

Before, that was all it had been to her. The ending of a wonderful movie, or a good book. The ending of an evening.

But on that knoll with Blake under a mellow sun, she discovered this kiss was not an ending. But a beginning.

For almost as fast as it had filled her, it now left her longing for more, longing to follow its heated path to the core of her own femininity, to the core of her own passion.

Her hands explored him, hungry for that more. Hungry to know him. She touched the hard muscles of his shoulders and his broad back with wonder that became delight that became more hunger. It wasn't enough to feel his back through his shirt. She wanted to touch his skin.

She became aware that his hands too were exploring, not with her urgency, though. Stroking her back, and her neck and her cheek, his power leashed, his wanting curbed.

His hands on her. Her hands on him. Their lips tangled together. It was a type of delicious sensory overload that obliterated all else. Soon sensation became everything.

Even the sky faded, the scent of crushed grass, and trees and the strawberries.

Her mind held only one thought, and it was a thought without words, a thought that went back to the beginnings of time and soared forward into the future.

If it had taken form it would have been: Know him.

In every way.

Know his lips and his touch, know how her own fingers reacted to his skin beneath them, and how that set off a chain reaction of shivers and tingles.

Know him.

Her body, her mind, her spirit united in this quest.

Know him.

In this new and wondrous way, know him.

Boldly, transforming into a woman she had not been before, she tugged his shirt out of his jeans, and sighed when she felt the silk of his skin beneath her fingertips.

"Holly."

It was part groan and part protest and part welcome. Lightly she ran her fingers over the smooth skin at the small of his back, allowed them to trail higher, trace the wings of his great shoulders, the muscles and ridges.

If she was blind, this is what braille would have been to her. The wonder that opened up a whole new world, a whole new dimension.

She would never ever be the same woman she had been ten minutes ago.

And then his lips left hers, and she felt him taking

her hands from his back, guiding them away from him.

She opened her eyes and looked at him.

He looked at her, tortured, torn. In his eyes she saw that he wanted her.

And in his face she saw that he was betraying something he held to be true by wanting her so desperately.

"What?" she whispered, stealing by the guard of his hands, touching him again.

He closed his eyes, gathering himself to say no to her.

"Blake, don't—"

But he did. He took her hand and put it gently away from him.

"We can't do this, Holly."

"Why?" She waited in terror. There was someone else. He didn't care about her in that way. He would never care about her in that way.

"It's wrong."

"Wrong?" Wrong as in against his religion. Did he have a religion? How could he call something that had been so right, wrong?

"Holly, I'm your boss."

"Oh. That kind of wrong. Against-your-principles wrong."

"Exactly."

She looked at him closely. Was that all it was? Or was it something more? Was that just his tactful way of letting her know it wasn't the same for him as it was for her?

She knew it couldn't be the same for him, because

she could not have stopped it. Not even with the considerable effort it had taken him.

She did not even want to stop it now, her desire at war with her pride. Part of her wanted to ignore him, fling herself at him, capture his lips again, use every bit of her feminine power to dispel his.

But when she looked at his face, she could not.

He was looking away from her, over the valley, something in his expression hard and cold and totally unapproachable.

"It must be hard being inside you," she said, and damned the shaking of her voice. "The renegade and the righteous sharing the same body."

He laughed a little. "It's very hard." Then he looked at her closely. "It must be hard being inside you—the innocent and the passionate sharing the same body."

"What makes you think I'm innocent?" That kiss had tempted something bolder, wilder to her surface. Somehow she thought it might have fooled him.

"Just a guess," he said, not at all fooled.

"I don't plan to be that way forever." It was possibly the boldest thing she had said in twenty-seven years. An unmistakable invitation.

Blake got off the blanket as if it had been invaded by ants, and began to pack things away. He wouldn't look at her.

Holly was devastated. There. She had tossed all the dice, she had not one single thing left.

And the answer was still no.

He glanced at her, and she saw the pity in his face. Pity. Just what every woman who had just brazenly offered herself to a man wanted to see.

"I have to do the ethical thing," he told her gently. "Do you understand that?"

"Of course," she said, getting up, turning away from him, pretending to brush crumbs from her clothing, when she was fighting not to cry.

"Holly, we can't do this. Do you understand? How can we work together, in the same office if we follow that path we were just on?"

"I understand perfectly." Somehow her moment had slipped away from her. She could see the resolution on his face, the determination.

Set against her.

She wondered if she crossed the distance between them if she could change that. With her lips, her body.

But suddenly she felt very uncertain herself, and did not feel strong enough to withstand another blow. She let him go ahead down the path, watched the grace of his walk with a longing that was intensified now that she had tasted him and touched him.

As they walked silently back toward the ranch, they could see from above a car pull into the driveway.

A white car. A big car.

Stephen Darce.

Blake's face was blacker than thunder.

"You can't have it both ways," she told him quietly. "You can't not have me, and have me, too."

"I know that."

"Then you have a decision to make."

"It's already made."

She looked at the strength in his face, the torment.

"I didn't tell him to come here," she said.

"It's okay. I know the feeling. He probably can't stay away."

She would not let that enigmatic statement give her hope. She would not. It was over. Before it had really begun, it was over.

Ten

Blake tried not to let his fury show as they approached the office, and Steve Darce stood waiting for them, leaning his fanny against the side of his car of his snow-white luxury car.

Blake slid Holly a look, trying to see how she felt about the banker. Or the car.

Her face was carefully blank.

But the banker's was not. Steve, who had that fresh-scrubbed boy scout look that Blake would never attain, not if he was respectable for a million years, looked from Holly to Blake to the picnic basket and back to Blake. Blake did nothing to dispel the uncomfortable understanding that dawned in Darce's eyes.

"I've come at a bad time," he said.

Blake said nothing.

But Holly, always the kind one, rushed to put him

at ease. "Of course you haven't, Steve. But what are you doing here?"

"I called your office earlier. When there was no answer I started to worry. You know with the water thing still unsolved—"

Darce's concern for Holly blackened a mood Blake would have sworn ten seconds ago could not get any darker. Plus, he wondered what exactly Holly had confided in Darce about the water. Had she told him about the bad dreams? Had he done more than pat her shoulder?

"Blake and I were just out of the office for a bit."

Blake shot her a look. Her hair was scattered around her head, her cheeks were on fire, and there were little bits of grass stuck in her sweater. The picnic basket was obviously depleted, and the neck of the bottle of wine stuck out of it. If Darce was dim enough not to get it, then he was going to go and withdraw all his money from the bank. Bankers were supposed to be smart.

"Thank you for being concerned, Steve," she said softly.

As if any man's brains could be expected to work properly after that.

"Look, since I'm here—" He shot Blake a look that let him know this was personal.

Blake stubbornly folded his arms over his chest and planted his feet apart.

"I need to talk to you." When it was obvious Blake wasn't moving, he leaned closer to her. "I got some tickets to 98 Degrees. They are very hard to come by. I wondered if you might like to go."

Blake was dimly aware, from working with teenagers, and teenage girls in particular that 98 Degrees was what was known as a "boy band." Good-looking guys who sang romantic music that gave girls the entirely erroneous impression that guys thought of relationships all the time, when in fact guys thought mostly about football stats, and motorcycle parts, and only managed to squeeze in the odd thought about women on the off chance that they might get lucky.

He hoped Holly would have the sense to know that band was not only too young for her, but that the message of that kind of music was hopelessly naive.

Steve Darce, however, looked like he might be thinking about Holly more than motorcycle parts, which made Blake want to go over to him, lift him up by his lapels and slam him against the car.

Even though, come to think of it, he had been thinking about her more than motorcycle parts himself.

She hesitated, and studied her toe rather than look at either of them. "When is it?"

That didn't sound like the out-and-out no Blake was hoping for. At all.

Steve named a date three weeks away, which Blake contemplated. It might be a good thing, in that Steve wasn't enthusiastic enough to be asking her about tonight or tomorrow. And it might be a bad thing in that Steve was obviously thinking about Holly long term.

"Can I think about it and get back to you?" she asked.

Steve gave Blake an accusing look as if he had spoiled a nice moment. Blake looked back at him unflinchingly. It gave him a certain satisfaction that Steve blinked first.

"Sure. That would be fine. And by the way, tomorrow is—"

Blake knew if he stayed here a moment longer he was not going to be responsible for what happened next. At least Darce had his glasses on today. Somewhere in that code of ethics that was causing Blake such grief, there was a rule about dealing with guys in glasses.

"Holly," he snapped, "I'm taking the rest of the day off. Cancel my afternoon appointments. And the conference call." He managed, just barely, not to be sarcastic about her conducting her personal business on the ranch dime, but only because they had just been consuming wine and exchanging kisses on the ranch dime themselves.

She gave him a surprised look, as if she was astounded he had a personal life.

Which he didn't.

Blake bypassed his office and went up the stairs to his apartment. His black leather jacket hung way back in his closet. There was dust on it. He slipped it on, and it felt like coming home.

She was at her desk, when he came back down the stairs, Darce nowhere in evidence. She was looking studiously at something on her computer. She raised a hand absently in farewell, then did a double take, looked quickly away, a blush rising in her cheeks.

So, she thought he looked great in black leather. She wasn't the first woman to share that weakness.

"I didn't know you had a motorcycle," she squeaked.

There. She didn't know the most important things about him.

"Didn't you?"

She shook her head. "I always wanted to try that."

Temptation reared its ugly head. Ask her. Ask her to play hooky with him, and spend a splendid day, with her arms wrapped around him, the wind tangling in her hair, her laughter in his ears.

Fallon, he told himself, you've played quite enough hooky for one day.

He managed to get out the door without giving in to the temptation that wrestled with bearlike strength within his brain. And moments later he had his big bike out of a back shed. It throbbed comfortably to life, just as if it had been yesterday he rode it, instead of six or seven months ago. He rode flat-out down country roads, losing track of time, outrunning the chaos and confusion inside of him. It was getting dark by the time he turned toward home, and he ached with weariness, a passable imposter for serenity.

Passing a little roadside bar that had excellent food, he saw Rafe's vehicle, and on impulse pulled over and went in. The lighting was dim, but he spotted Rafe at a booth in the corner.

He'd forgotten that Libby was a part of the Rafe equation now. They were just finishing dinner. Blake wanted to talk to Rafe. He really didn't want a woman's take on the events of the afternoon. He turned to leave, but Rafe suddenly spotted him and did a double take that reminded him of Holly's earlier.

"Hey, Renegade!" Rafe motioned him over. "Are

you out on your bike? I can't believe it. I haven't seen you ride that old hog for ages.''

Libby seemed to sense Blake's need, because after a minimum of chitchat she glanced suddenly at her watch and gave a little cry of dismay.

"I have an appointment," she said. "Rafe, I'll see you later. Blake, good seeing you again."

Something smoldered in both their eyes, and Blake had the feeling that Rafe was thinking way too much about things other than football stats and motorcycle parts himself. Blake felt this furious flash of envy that tonight Rafe was not going to bed alone.

And if he had played his damn cards right he wouldn't be either.

"You want to talk?" Rafe asked, gesturing to the abandoned seat at the booth.

"No," Blake snapped.

"Okay, you want to play some pool?"

"That sounds more like it."

It was after Blake had missed every shot that Rafe said, "You might as well tell me."

"Tell you what?" Blake said defensively.

"You haven't missed shots like those since you were nine years old."

"So, I'm having an off day."

"And I haven't seen that particular look on your face for a long time either."

"What look is that?"

"It's a kind of I'm-looking-for-an-excuse-to-bust-somebody's-face look. Along with the black leather, it's a pretty menacing combination. It seems to have scared Libby into the next county."

"Sorry," he muttered.

"Just tell me. It can't be any worse than some of your other stuff. I know everything bad there is to know about you, remember? You can't shock me, offend me or scare me."

Blake leaned on his pool cue. "I kissed my secretary today."

Rafe flubbed the shot, turned and looked at him over his shoulder. "Was it good?"

"That's not the point!"

"It's not? You're up."

Blake took a clean miss on a simple bank shot. "A boss can't kiss his secretary."

"You mean, there she was filing papers and you snuck up behind her and whirled her around, bent her over backward and kissed her while she screamed and flailed at you?" Rafe chalked his cue, blew the dust off, regarded Blake over the top of it.

"No. We were, um, on a picnic."

"A picnic?"

Neither man was even pretending to play pool anymore.

"She packed a picnic." He put enough swear words between "a" and "picnic" to make a sailor blush.

But Rafe only laughed. "*She* packed a picnic?"

"Yeah."

"Like what? Peanut butter sandwiches?"

"Not exactly."

"Tell me. Exactly."

"Cheese, strawberries, wine. Stuff like that."

"I'm no expert, but if Libby packed me a lunch like that, she'd expect me to kiss her."

"Holly isn't Libby."

"Same species."

"Even if that is what she expected, that doesn't make it right."

"In what way?"

"I'm her boss."

"Wasn't this bugging you at the dance the other night?"

He wanted to deny it. He couldn't.

"I'll tell you again, Blake, you're taking the Dudley-do-Right thing a little too far. You've already outrun your misspent youth. And just because your dad took a shot at somebody doesn't mean you have to keep proving you're lily white. We all know you aren't capable of doing anything even remotely naughty from littering to going too fast on your motorcycle to kissing your secretary."

"If anybody else said that, they'd be on the floor," Blake said tersely.

"It's probably why so few people are willing to tell you the truth. Look, you've wanted to hit somebody since you came in here. It might as well be me—at least I won't press charges. Who knows? I might take you."

Blake felt the darkness lighten and smiled with self-mocking. "That would be a first."

"You want some advice?"

"No."

"Yes, you do. That's why you came in here when you saw my vehicle."

"All right," Blake snapped. "As if I've ever been able to stop you from talking once you've got your mind set to it."

"Come out of the dark ages."

"Pardon?"

"In your non-relationship with your secretary, you have all the power, according to you."

"And I don't want to abuse it," Blake said, stung by the non-relationship comment.

"It's abuse when she doesn't have a choice. Say if you were making unwanted passes at her, pinching her behind when she walked by, peering down her shirt, accidentally brushing her curves. That would be an abuse of power. There's the I'm-gonna-cream-somebody look again, and I'm the only one here. Calm down, Blake. I know you aren't acting like that, for God's sake. I'm explaining something.

"A more subtle abuse of power is not allowing her to make choices. You're going to be the one totally in control all the time. From what I've seen of Holly, she is quite capable of making good choices for herself. Maybe, as unthinkable as it seems to me when I look at your ugly mug, she wants you. I mean, why else a picnic lunch?"

Blake thought about the picnic lunch, the cookies, the flowers.

Rafe continued. "She gave out the signal, not you. So, ask her out. The choice is hers. If she says no, then absolutely no forcing kisses upon her behind the filing cabinet. If she says yes…" Rafe shrugged wickedly.

Blake stared at him. Could it be that simple? Could this ethical struggle he'd been involved in be a non-issue?

"Blake, is it really about being a good boss, or is this *it?*"

"It?"

"*It.* You know, the one. The first woman who's ever got through that tough shell of yours, the first one who has made you realize what intimacy can be."

Blake sensed a frightening truth in that. Holly, his plain little secretary, had snuck by his defenses when he wasn't looking. He had never guarded his heart against her. Maybe would not have been able to if he tried.

Because she was so different than all the other women he had known.

Deep. Compassionate. Funny. Smart. Warm.

She filled some hole in him that no one had ever come close to even touching before. Rafe had hit the nail on the head.

He wasn't worried about being a good boss.

He was worried about surrendering his soul.

"I'm going to tell you something in total confidence, Blake."

Blake eyed him warily.

"She needs you right now. She's going to need someone strong to stand by her."

"Why?"

"I can't tell you."

"Hey, I just spilled my guts to you."

"Trust me on this one. It's better that you don't know. If you ran off half-cocked right now, months of hard work could be jeopardized."

"You know who poisoned the water," Blake guessed in a low, threatening growl.

"I might."

Blake knew if Rafe had decided not to tell him he was never going to get it out of him. Never. Perhaps that was one of the reasons they had remained good friends for so many years. Because that same band of steel-hard stubbornness ran through both of them.

"What's it got to do with Holly?"

Rafe ran a hand through his hair. "I told you, I'm not telling you. But I'll tell you this: If you have feelings for her, you don't have time to debate it for another few months, deciding what's wrong and what's right. She's going to need you to be there for her now. Right now. Within days."

"I hope she's not going to be too disappointed about 98 Degrees," Blake muttered.

"What?"

"Nothing," Blake said, putting down his pool cue. "I've got to go."

"Good luck, buddy," Rafe said softly.

Her light was still on when he pulled up on his motorcycle. He shut it off in front of her cabin and took the steps two at a time. He pounded on her door. "Holly!"

She came and opened it a crack, and peeped around it. He'd been right about the nightgown. Straight out of *Little House on the Prairie*. White, sweeping the floor, little ruffles at the high neckline and at the cuffs around the sleeves. How could something so prim be so damned sexy?

He looked hard at her. For somebody who was supposed to be excited about a concert she looked like she'd been crying.

"Hi," he said casually, as if it wasn't nearly midnight.

"Hi," she said.

"Did I wake you up? I thought I saw a light."

"No, you didn't wake me."

"Can I come in? Just for a second?"

"Uh—"

"I'll wait. If you want to throw on a pair of jeans or something."

She wanted to say no. He could tell. He'd hurt her quite enough for one day. But she didn't say no. She nodded and closed the door.

He stood on the porch, went to the edge of it and looked at the sky.

It felt like he had never seen stars before. Ever. The air felt velvety and warm.

He heard the door whisper open behind him, and turned back. She had pulled a robe over the nightgown, knotted it at the waist.

He felt like he was looking at the future. The way she would look puttering around the house on a Sunday morning. Or when he brought her tea and the newspaper in bed.

He was asking her on a date, he reminded himself roughly, not to marry him.

She held open the door, and he went through it. He had seen her place once before, when he had picked her up for the dance.

It looked different tonight. She was burning candles, and it looked soft and welcoming, like a place a man who had been running all his life could take his heart to rest.

If she said yes.

If she made the choice.

"I was wrong," he said, looking down at her, fighting hard the urge to take her in his arms, pull her to him, taste her lips again.

"Wrong?" she asked.

"About it being wrong."

Her eyes widened. "I'm not sure I'm following you."

"I told you it was wrong. That kiss on the hill today."

"Oh," she said, and even in the soft glow of the candlelight he could see the blush moving up her cheeks, staining them the most beautiful shade of pink.

"If you'll give me a chance, I want to try this again. Not me boss, you secretary. But me man, you woman." God, he thought he sounded like Tarzan.

Her mouth worked for a moment, but not a sound came out. Were those tears sparkling in her eyes? He was making a complete mess of this, but he plunged stubbornly ahead anyway, a man who had decided to navigate quicksand, even though he knew fully the risks.

"I don't want it to be like asking you to the dance. It's not to thank you for the wonderful job you do of looking after me in the office. It's got nothing to do with the office. I'd like to take you out. Because I like you. Because I want to know you better."

For the longest time he thought he'd blown it, her silence stretched so long.

"I want," he finally said, "for the choice to be yours. Will you go out with me?"

"Yes," she whispered.

Suddenly he wished they could just skip all the next part. Going out together. Awkwardly holding hands during a movie, sharing buttered popcorn, slipping his hand over her shoulder.

He wanted to just get to the part where his lips were on her lips again. And other parts of her, too.

He reminded himself he did a fair imitation of a civilized man now.

And besides, this was Holly. Decent, wholesome Holly.

"So," he said, "maybe a movie tomorrow night?"

Did she look disappointed?

"Unless you have a better idea," he said, remembering what Rafe had said about sharing power, giving her choice.

Her whole face brightened up. "What I'd really like to do is go for a motorcycle ride. Could we do that?"

Why hadn't he thought of that?

"Sure," he said. "We could do that. There's a nice little inn about thirty miles north of here on the secondary highway. We could go there for dinner and come back."

"That sounds perfect."

He could leave now, but he didn't.

The tension was suddenly in the room. Electrical. Sensual. That kiss of this afternoon whispered on the air between them. He wondered if her lips would still taste of strawberries.

He stepped toward her.

Her eyes were wide and reminded him so poignantly of what he had tasted in that kiss, besides strawberries.

Innocence.

That was the part he'd forgotten to discuss with Rafe. Holly's innocence in the face of his experience.

"I'll pick you up around five. Do you have a leather jacket?"

"No."

"I'll see what I can dig up for you. I probably have one I've outgrown somewhere." The one he'd stolen when he was fourteen would fit her perfectly. It was probably a measure of his true character that he still had a soft spot for that jacket.

Now he could leave. He still didn't. He took another step toward her. And then another. And then he dropped his head and tasted her lips.

Not strawberries anymore.

They tasted like rain. Clean and pure.

Before he totally lost his head, he spun on his heel and went out the door. And ordered himself to think of motorcycle parts and football stats until five o'clock tomorrow.

But somehow he already knew he wasn't going to listen.

Eleven

Holly touched her lips and stared at the door that had just closed behind Blake. The smell of his leather jacket, tangy and rich, still filled the air of her small cottage, swirled around her like an embrace.

All she could think was that dreams, those elusive wisps of hope and magic that she had been about to pack away and hide under her bed for good, came true for ordinary girls like her, after all.

Blake had asked her out, and he couldn't have been more plain. His interest in her was pure and potently masculine.

The taste of his lips was still on hers, and she touched her tongue to her own lips and felt joyful and afraid and joyful again. Could he love her? Could a man like Blake Fallon ever love a woman like her?

She reminded herself firmly that it was a date, not a declaration of love.

But when she remembered the smoldering look in his gray eyes, she shivered and hugged herself.

She spent the entire next day on pins and needles like a bride before her wedding. She tried on different outfits and fiddled with her makeup and played with her hair.

But in the end she had to concede to the reality she had created: She was going to be on a motorcycle. Which meant that navy blue skirt that always got such a nice reaction at the office was out. And so was too much makeup as the wind would be blowing in her face. If her eyes teared, she didn't want mascara running down her cheeks. And as for her hair, there was no sense going to great lengths for that either, because she would be wearing a helmet that would squish whatever she did anyway.

She ended up wearing her new green shirt and a pair of jeans, flat sensible shoes and just the faintest touch of makeup. She left her hair loose.

She tried to read. She tried to clean her house. She tried to knit.

But she could not make the time fly by until he got there. It was a humbling experience because Holly had always secretly scorned women who went to bits over men, who put their own lives on a shelf for the latest beau.

But then, with a gentleness born of the love blossoming within her, Holly forgave herself. This wasn't her *latest* beau. This was her *only* beau.

This was the first time she had ever been in the grip of these wonderful and terrifying emotions and she knew she had to give herself a little leeway. Even the most practical of women were entitled to lose their heads once in a while.

Once in a lifetime.

And that was how she felt when she finally heard the motorcycle stop outside her house. Like she had completely lost her head. She wanted to run and change clothes. She wanted to run to the mirror and do a final check. She wanted to hide under the bed. No, she wanted to fling herself into his arms. How could two such wildly opposing thoughts hold court in the same brain?

The knock came at the door. Firm and strong.

She felt giddy and hot and cold, and she wished she had never started this, and was so glad that she had.

She took a deep, steadying breath and went to the door and opened it.

And amazingly, just like that, she felt just right.

He was wearing his black leather jacket and faded jeans, and his hair fell boyishly over his forehead. His gray eyes took her in, and a light winked on in them.

"I brought you this." He held up the jacket for her, and she turned around and slipped her arms into it.

It fit her like a black leather glove, and it had a tantalizing aroma to it. Leather, but something more. The boy he used to be clung to that jacket, wild and rebellious and devil-may-care. She snuggled into it.

"Nice fit," he said, turning her around and eyeing her with frank male appreciation.

Her. Holly Lamb.

Then he kissed her, on the tip of her nose, and

leaned back, smiling. "You look great in black leather. I never figured you for a wild kind of girl."

Somehow she knew he was going to coax the wild side of her to the surface. Maybe she had always known that, and it had formed part of the irresistible attraction she felt for him.

He waited while she locked the door to her house, and they walked down the steps together.

He had two helmets on the seat of the motorbike, and he took one off and crooked a finger at her.

She stepped close to him, and he set it down on her head and guided it over her ears. Carefully, he took the wisps of her hair that were sticking out and tucked them up under, before he took the chin strap and pulled it tight, snapped it closed.

The whole time, she looked at him, felt his touch, felt some trembling begin within her.

He put his own helmet on, then mounted the motorcycle first, swinging his long legs over it, kicking down hard to start it. She saw the muscle in his leg ripple when he did that, and tremble deepened into anticipation.

He patted the seat behind him, and she climbed on, suddenly shy about what to do with her hands, her legs.

She settled for holding the back of the seat; her heels found the passenger bar.

But he turned and over his shoulder gave a small shake of his head. He reached back with one arm and pulled her right into him, so her chest was flattened against the black leather of his broad back, her thighs making an intimate V around his rear end. Lastly, he took her arms and guided them around his waist.

"Hold on tight," he ordered.

He gave the big machine a bit of juice, and the deep, rumbling purr it was making turned to a roar, and it surged smoothly forward. One leg down, he made a smooth circle to turn around, then put his leg up and gave the bike more gas.

They headed out on the highway, a paved back road that twisted and turned through the abundant beauty of redwood country.

But the truth was the scenery was lost on Holly.

Her cheek on his back, her arms around him, her body finding the rhythm of the bike so that she leaned when he leaned and came back to center when he did, was exhilarating, like learning the steps of a dance. He blocked the worst of the wind, but still she could feel it on her cheeks, trying to tug her hair out from under the helmet.

She felt alive. And free. And on fire.

She laughed into the wind, held tighter with her arms and called, "Faster."

He glanced back at her, grinned and opened the bike up. They surged around twists in the road, soared through dips and hollows. She thought that this, not being in an airplane, was probably as close as human beings could ever come to knowing what it was to fly.

It seemed too soon when he came to the little country inn that he had promised, though when the bike stopped she realized her hands were cold, and so were her cheeks.

She slid off and blew on her hands.

Seeing that, he came and took them in his. "Next time I'll remember gloves," he said.

Next time. Two small words. Beautiful words.

"Did you like it?" he asked.

"Like it?" The words seemed so inadequate. "It gives new meaning to the word freedom."

He looked at her thoughtfully, smiled a small smile. "Exactly." He held her hands flat between the two of his, until she could feel the blood flowing back into her fingertips. Then he tucked her hand in his and escorted her into the restaurant.

It was a small, cozy place, with lace at the French-paned windows and a mismatch of antique chairs and tables.

They were led to a quiet table in the corner, where a candle flickered in a glass globe.

"Good," she said. "Darkness. You can't see my hair."

He laughed, ran a hand through his own hair. "The price of freedom. But you should see your cheeks. You're blushing like a—" he stopped, and something grew very dark in his eyes, as if it occurred to him the circumstances under which brides blushed. "A tomato," he finished insincerely.

"A tomato?" she sputtered, and then they were laughing together, and it felt so good. The way it had been before, only better. The way it had been before, only with an exciting new dimension, an exciting new possibility, shimmering on the air with their laughter.

Over a delicious dinner, he proved himself to be every bit the man she had always known he was. He was tender and funny and strong.

And to her amazement he was vulnerable.

He told her about the first time he'd been locked up. Just a little boy who'd stolen a bicycle. The policeman, wanting to throw a scare into him, had put him into a cell until his mom, annoyed about being disturbed at a luncheon, finally came for him.

"Funny, isn't it?" he said softly. "When I heard that door click closed, I swore that would never happen to me again. That feeling of being trapped, of being totally in someone else's power, is terrifying. But somehow having my mother's full and undivided attention made it all worthwhile. Or maybe I never got good at thinking an action through to its consequence. Maybe I'm still not that good at that."

And the way he was looking at her, she knew he was talking about this. The motorbike ride and the dinner. Had either of them thought where this was leading?

In her wildest dreams, she had.

"I've heard you say it to the boys in The Shack a million times. Think it all the way through. Right to the end."

And as soon as she said those words, it was like it was on the table between them. The need and the passion.

The way this evening was going to end.

His hand covered hers, and he lifted it to his lips and kissed it, long and slow until it felt like her blood was coming to a slow boil, and her skin would melt away from her body. Nothing had ever interested her less than dessert.

Without another word, he got up and helped her into her jacket, his hands lingering on her shoulders. He paid the check, and they left.

Night had fallen, the stars hanging in the sky, huge and bright.

"Put your hands in my jacket pockets," he said.

But she didn't. She slid her hands around him and right between the snaps on his jacket, so that her hands rested right under his rib cage and she could feel the steady rise and fall of his breath, the heat of his body.

He turned and gave her a look that was part pleasure and part pain, and then he stoked up the big bike and they headed back down the road where they had come.

Only everything was different now.

The road was only a path to somewhere else, necessary miles that had to be covered. The path ended at her cabin door, where a light left on burned softly within.

The words had dried up between them.

She took his hand to lead him up the stairs, but he pulled her into him, carefully unbuckled the helmet, slid it off her head, dropped it to the ground, and did the same to his.

His hands on either side of her face, he guided her lips to his, and tasted her with a savage hunger. One powerful leg nudged between hers, and she wantonly pressed herself into the steel of his thigh.

"Are you coming in?" she whispered breathlessly.

"Unless you're planning on doing it out here," he said. She knew what her eyes said, as they lingered on his face with hunger.

He scooped her up and went up the steps, while she kissed his chin and his chest and anything else within range of her lips.

"Give me the damn keys," he growled huskily.

Laughing as he balanced her weight and managed

the door, she allowed herself to revel in his strength, in the feel of steel-hard muscles supporting her thighs and shoulders.

He finally kicked the door open, went unerringly to her bedroom door, partly ajar, and shoved it open, too.

He dropped her on the pure white bedspread, looked down at her while she gazed helplessly up at him, unaware how sensual was the contrast between her pristine white eyelet spread and the black leather jacket she still wore.

He was everything men had ever been. He was a hunter and a warrior and a pirate and a king. His breath was rising raggedly, swelling his chest. He gazed at her with tenderness and wanting and power and passion.

He was every man who had ever come to a woman and laid his weapons and his power at her feet.

She opened her arms and he came to her, holding the majority of his weight off of her, while he tasted the softness of her eyelids, the tip of her nose. He nipped the lobes of her ears and ran his tongue, like a sword of intense fire, down the tender curve of her neck.

His questing mouth was like an exquisite form of torture.

''Blake.'' She whispered his name, and heard the shocking urgency in her voice. She wanted to beg him to kiss deeper, hold harder, move faster.

He put a finger to her lips, silencing her, and continued his slow, torturing nuzzle, his lips on her breastbone, his eyes suddenly intent on her face.

His hand slid underneath the opened black leather

jacket to the button of her jade green blouse, and he stopped, gazed at her, teased the button with his fingertip, a small smile on his lips, the question in his eyes.

"Yes," she said hoarsely in answer.

He flicked the button free, his eyes still on her face, touched the pale skin beneath it, lightly, ever so lightly, with the tip of his finger. And then he dropped his head to where his finger had been, and touched the silken flesh between her breasts with his lips, and then his tongue.

With a flame leaping in his eyes that he leashed in the unhurried touch of his hands, he slowly undid each of the buttons on her blouse, anointing with his lips the tender flesh he exposed before moving on to the next button.

Holly had never felt such exquisite agony as this slow, painstaking uncovering.

The blouse was undone. Never taking his eyes from her face, he placed his hands on either side of the placket, and tugged it gently open. Finally, when she thought she might scream with wanting and frustration, his gaze dropped, heated, to what he had uncovered.

He tugged the sleeves over her shoulders, pulling both the blouse and the jacket free, dropped them carelessly to the floor. He shrugged off his own jacket before he ran a fingertip over the lacy cup that held one breast and then the other, and then he touched the place where her tender flesh mounded over the top of her bra.

She was gasping at each new path of fire his fingertips forged over her skin, but he would not be rushed in his lazy exploration of her. He could not know this was her first time, and yet he seemed determined to make it an experience that would last forever, be unforgettable.

He bent over her and ran his hot tongue down a line from just below her breast to her belly button. He stopped there for a moment, kissed, probed that slight hollow with the spear of his tongue, then kissed a tantalizing line at the waistband of her jeans.

He paused again at the snap, looking at her, his eyes dark with wicked amusement at her longing, but his own ragged breathing revealing he was not nearly as calm or in control as his slow exploration of her might have her believe.

His hand rested, heavy and warm, on the fabric below that snap. When she thrust herself into the hand, he smiled, flicked the snap open, eased the zipper down, ran fingers over lace, like a pianist doing feather-light scales. And then, while his mouth breathed fire onto that same lace, his hands took purchase of the fabric at her hips and tugged.

The jeans slid off her and hit the floor.

"Your turn," he said huskily, drawing a circle on the skin of her inner thigh with his fingertips.

"My turn?" she said. She didn't even know she got a turn, let alone what she was supposed to do with it.

"Take my shirt off, Holly."

He leaned over her, and stilled her fingers when she shoved the first button through the hole and made her way to the second one.

"Slowly," he commanded her, even though his arms trembled from holding himself above her.

She was trembling now, too, as her fingers found each button, as she did as he had done and kissed the flesh that she exposed, touched it with her lips and her tongue, felt the exquisite warmth radiating from him, felt the muscles of his chest, the corded muscles on his belly.

She wondered if it was possible to faint with wanting.

The buttons finally all open, she drew the shirt away from him, and touched and kissed, and touched some more. She found the hard nub of his nipple, touched it, squirmed beneath him so that she could reach it with her tongue. She circled it, flicked it, and then gently nipped it.

For the first time, he groaned. And then he knelt over her, his blue-jean clad thighs on either side of her stomach, and shrugged off his shirt.

She stared at him, her senses feasting on the masculine perfection of his body. But when she reached to touch him again, he caught her hands and guided them to the snap on his jeans.

She undid the snap. Her fingers trembling, she touched his zipper, eased it down, felt the heat and hardness beneath her fingertips. He shoved the blue jeans down, moved to the edge of the bed and tore them off his legs.

He stretched out on the bed beside her, unselfconscious in only navy blue jockey shorts, the white band brilliant against the faint copper tones of his skin. She thought he looked like a swimmer—broad shoulders, flat stomach, narrow hips, long, strong legs.

He was on his stomach, propped up on his elbow.

He reached out with his free arm, his hand flat, and caressed her skin with his palm, from her breastbone to her belly button. She shuddered, his hand the quake, her body the aftershock.

"I love the way you feel," he whispered. "Soft. Sacred."

Sacred. That was the word, exactly, that described what was happening between them, the unfolding of this great and powerful intimacy that had celebrated man and woman since the beginning of time.

Lost in that power, Holly Lamb became everything she had never been.

She had been shy, now she became bold.

She had been cautious, now she became adventurous.

She had never taken risks, and now she felt prepared to risk it all.

"Blake," she whispered, her voice ragged with need, her patience spent. "I want you. I want you now."

He smiled, lifted his weight on top of her and settled it. And then he kissed her. There was nothing sweet in his kisses now. The tender exploratory nature of them melted like sugar into hot water.

The mouth that claimed hers was hard, commanding, urgent.

His hands on her body became less tender, and more possessive, a man claiming what was his, claiming what was being offered to him, saying a resounding yes to the gifts of the universe and the mysteries of life.

He undid the clasp on her bra and watched, his eyes dark, his mouth unsmiling, as her breasts sprang free.

And then his lips and tongue rained fire on her, nipping, kissing, licking, tenderness giving way to raw need.

She arched into the fiery hail of his lips. A sound came from her own lips, a sound that welled up from within her. It was a sound of need and desire and pleasure and pain, those things so related that they were no longer separate.

He slid her lace panties over a slender hip and slid down the silken length of an unresisting thigh. She wriggled them the rest of the way down and tossed them on the floor with her toe.

She was naked beneath the man she loved.

His hand caressed the soft flesh of her inner thigh, tangled in the curl of her hair, stroked the place between her legs that had turned silky with moisture.

She was crazed. Her nails bit into his shoulders, and she pulled herself hard against him, loving the scrape of her breasts against the springy hair on his chest. Her body took on a life of its own, writhing, bucking, begging.

And then the last barrier, his undershorts, were gone. He paused for just a moment, protecting her, and then holding himself up again over her body, his elbows locked and his arms trembling, he nudged her legs apart and slipped inside her.

She was taken aback by the sudden pain, and she saw him stop, saw the shock on his face as he registered what had just happened.

He looked, for an awful second, like he was going to withdraw from her.

"This is what I want," she said, her voice fierce. "It's my choice."

He lowered himself from his elbows, gathered her to him, whispered in her ear that she was beautiful, and then, gently, he pushed and pierced the silken thread of her innocence.

When she cried out, he stopped, brushed the hair from her eyes, kissed her cheeks, and then slowly, thrust again.

Like that, the pain was gone, and she was lifted up to a different plane. A wild throbbing began at her core, and instead of retreating from him, she met him. She wrapped her arms tighter around his neck, and found her legs wrapping themselves around the hard curves of his waist.

They rode the crashing waves in perfect unison, until they crested.

An explosion went off inside of her, tiny like the first small pop of a firecracker on the Fourth of July. But the one that followed was more intense, and then came another, until they were coming so rapidly, one on top of the other, each explosion more powerful than the last, until with an exultant cry of fulfillment, she went limp in his arms.

When she dared open her eyes, he was staring at her with absolute and utter amazement. His smile was slow and sexy and warm, as he brushed the sweat-drenched hair from her forehead.

He gathered her to him and rocked her, as her joyous tears began to fall.

Twelve

The tears chased down her cheeks, streaks of silver in the moonlit room. Blake kissed them away. They tasted of salt and dew and softness.

"I'm so sorry," he whispered, agonized. "I didn't mean to hurt you."

"Hurt me?" She hiccuped and laughed. "I'm crying because I'm happy."

He tilted his head back and looked at her, saw the glow in her eyes, the high color in her cheeks, the smile, and he knew it was true. She was happy. Deliriously, blissfully.

"I've never heard that line in real life—that people cry when they're happy," he admitted, smiling. "I thought it was something Hollywood made up."

"It's like there's so much emotion in me right now, my body can't hold it. The tears are the overflow valve. Pure paradise. It's too big to keep inside of me.'' She sighed and leaned her head against his chest. Her hands, almost unconsciously, moved over the muscles in his chest and arms, giving him the heady feeling she could not get enough of him.

"Nothing," she murmured, "could have prepared me for this experience. I mean, I've read about it and seen a whole lot in movies, but nothing can come close to experiencing what that's like. No wonder I was a virgin so long. I had no idea."

"You should have told me," he said, gathering her to him, secretly thrilled that she had had no idea and that this gift had become his.

"Really? Exactly how do you broach that subject? 'Blake, while I'm filing under V, I've suddenly recalled my virginity'?"

He laughed. "How about 'Blake, take it easy. I've never done this before.' Actually, I think I probably should have guessed. Maybe even had guessed, and then in the heat of the moment, managed to forget."

"How embarrassing. You guessed? Do you want the whole humiliating truth? I'm a wallflower. I've never even had a boyfriend, let alone been intimate before."

He didn't think she should find that truth embarrassing. It certainly wasn't her fault that the male populace was completely blind when it came to most things that mattered. The fact that she had never had a boyfriend rather endeared her to him, made him feel protective and possessive in ways he had not felt either of those things before.

"I just might have changed a few things, if you'd warned me," he reassured her.

"Exactly!" she said. "And I wouldn't change one single thing about what just happened between us."

"Come to think of it, neither would I." He kissed her again, tasted the sweetness of her lips. "They were wrong," he told her, "Every one of those guys who passed you by was wrong, and I'm so glad. I have a feeling you're going to show me all kinds of things I've never known before."

"Me show you? *You're* going to show *me* all kinds of things I've never known before," she said, tracing his lips with her fingers. "Riding the motorcycle was a first, too."

"Which was better?" he growled.

"The motorcycle," she said, deadpan, and then cracked up laughing at the look on his face. He liked her laughter so much, it was a temptation to tickle her or pull faces just to keep her laughing. But he had a better idea.

"Are you ready for another first?" he asked her softly.

"If you stay here tonight, and I fall asleep in your arms, that will be a first," she said, with a certain bewitching shyness.

"Oh, you're stuck with me for the night," he told her, and didn't add *at least*. He didn't want to scare her away.

He wagged his eyebrows at her, leaned toward her and whispered in her ear, "I bet you've never showered with a man before."

Her eyes went very wide, and her shyness seemed to deepen. She blushed crimson. After all they had just done together!

"Come on," he coaxed. "You have no idea how much fun a shower can be."

"Blake," she pulled the covers right over her head, "I'm not sure I'm ready for that. I mean, it's dark in here at least."

"I know," he said, pulling the covers off her head, "I don't see the darkness as a good thing. I want to see you. All of you. And touch you."

"Oh, God," she moaned, and tried to get back under the covers.

"I want to cover you with soap and run my hands all over you," he told her, not letting her burrow out of his sight.

She couldn't hide the fact she was intrigued. "Maybe I'll do it. Under certain conditions. Can I keep my eyes closed?"

He sighed patiently. "No. How would you see me, all of me, if your eyes were closed? Plus, you might get soap in my eyes."

He remembered thinking over dinner that she had been blushing like a bride. He'd been mistaken. *This* blush was a bridal blush. She was shy and excited and exhilarated, and maybe a little ashamed of that glorious vessel that was her body.

She probably thought her thighs were too fat or her breasts were too small, and that wouldn't do at all.

He couldn't wait to convince her how perfect she was. He tugged her hand and flipped the covers back.

She squeaked and tried to get back under them.

"You're beautiful," he assured her. "Come on. Take a risk."

She snatched back the sheet. "Do you have any

idea how many of those I've taken in the last few weeks?''

He smiled. "Great. That means you're getting good at it." He kissed her hand. "Come on."

She hesitated, debated, finally smiled. "All right."

He knew this was a fragile thing she was giving him, her trust. She hung behind him as he led her across the darkened bedroom to the ensuite. When he let go of her hand to switch on the light, she snatched a big white towel and wrapped it around herself.

He pretended to ignore her, adjusted the water, stepped under the hot spray. And then he reached out, yanked the towel away and took her hand and propelled her into the shower. He held her hard against him, as the water cascaded around them.

"You are beautiful," he told her sternly. "Absolutely gorgeous."

She sputtered indignantly for a few seconds, and then went very still against him.

"Oh, my," she said, as he moved his shoulders and slid his wet chest against the sweet curve of her breasts.

He reached for the soap, lathered it in his hands, and then, using large circular motions, began to wash her back, feeling the wet, beautiful slipperiness of her skin beneath his hands. She tucked in closer to him, but when he allowed his lathered hands to slip down to the delightful full curve of her buttocks, he felt her react, push herself into him.

He took it as a cue and stepped back from her. Slowly and with great tenderness, he soaped her breasts, her tummy. He knelt at her feet and soaped the length of her legs, and the miraculous place between them. He drank in her femininity, worshiped it, with his eyes and his touch and his senses. He let the water wash the soap away, trailed his lips over her rain-clean skin.

"Open your eyes," he told her over the drumming of the water, rising.

She did, lifted her chin, her gaze glued on his face, trying so hard not to look anywhere else.

He handed her the soap and folded her hand around it.

"Your turn."

She gasped slightly, looked down at the soap in her hand, closed her eyes again and gulped.

"It's easy," he said, and guided her hand to his shoulder.

And then tentatively she touched him, worked the soapy lather into the slope of his shoulders, moved to the hair on his chest, kissed his pectoral muscles, moved on to his belly.

Her hands, gloved in the soap, brought him as close to heaven as he knew he was ever going to be on this earth.

She made him turn around and she soaped his back.

Her hands, her touch, held innocence and reverence and eagerness. Her fingers were tentative, gentle, unknowingly sensuous, growing more and more certain as she gave herself permission to touch him, to know him in this way.

She stopped and he turned back to face her. Her eyes were wide open now, the water sliding over the silken ribbons of her hair, cascading over the fullness of her breasts, beading on the slender hollow of her stomach, catching like dew in that tangled triangle of temptation between her legs.

"You missed a place," he told her softly.

She hesitated, and then her hands, the soap, found him. He groaned, gathered her in his embrace, let his tongue find and taste the clean wet surfaces of her skin. The water pounded down on them, and the shower stall filled with a warm, sultry mist, cloaking them.

He had never made love in a shower before.

He didn't even know if it was possible. But it wasn't fair to ask her to be the only one taking risks. Her arms wound around his neck, and he lifted her up, amazed by how light she was, amazed again when her legs went around him.

With the water beating down on them, his muscles straining to keep them both from crashing to the floor of the bathtub, one arm braced against the shower stall wall, and the other holding her fast to him, he found out all things are possible.

The water turned cold without warning, and Blake managed to slam down the lever that stopped it from flowing out the shower head. The icy water cascaded out the tap and over his feet, but he was oblivious to it.

He and Holly reached crescendo at exactly the same time.

Gently he set her down outside the tub, jumped out and wrapped her in the big towel. She opened it, and he stood in the folds with her. Her teeth were rattling, so he pulled the towel tighter around them, used his body heat to warm her.

When the worst of her shivering had stopped, he reached for another towel, dried every inch of her.

And then he handed her the towel.

And she dried every inch of him.

And by the time they were done, her shyness had gone, and the heat had risen between them again to nearly fever pitch.

"Race you back to bed," he said.

Laughing, unselfconscious, as uninhibited as a woodland nymph, she darted out of the bathroom and across the cold, rough floor. He was right on her heels when she took a flying leap into the bed, and he landed right beside her.

He took her lips and kissed her until she was breathless once again, her breast heaving against his naked chest.

"Are we going to get any sleep tonight?" she asked playfully, nipping at his ear with her straight, white teeth.

"I certainly hope not," he answered.

But she did sleep after that, in fact she fell asleep with the easy and utter exhaustion of a small child who had spent the day at the beach.

Blake looked at her, her hair scattered across the pillow, her lashes casting small shadows on the roundness of her cheeks, and he marveled.

Who would have ever thought? But the black leather jacket against the white eyelet bedcover should have been his first clue. All Holly Lamb's secrets had been in those startlingly sensual contrasts when he had first tossed her on the bed.

A virgin hiding a tigress at her core.

He knew now the part of Holly Lamb that no one

who had ever looked at his prim and proper secretary would have ever guessed at.

Including himself.

The evening they had just spent together had taught him something that he hoped never to forget. That you could think you knew everything there was to know about something, and you might not know it at all.

He had thought, in his arrogance, he knew a thing or two about making love.

And found out what he knew about was sex. More accurately, what he knew about was the four-letter word that guys used so openly in the company of other guys, that word that was flung around so casually and abundantly in pool halls and taverns and the places with bars and locks where Blake had learned the language of being a certain kind of man.

That word had nothing to do with what had happened here tonight.

Or the kind of man he had seen reflected in the wonder in her eyes.

In her innocence and her awe, she had shown him what making love was about. It wasn't about a physical release.

It was about a spiritual joining.

It wasn't about some emptiness, longing to be filled.

It was about a lonely soul making its way unerringly toward completion.

Imagine. Educated about making love at the hands of Holly Lamb.

He thought of her hands and could feel his heat rising. Again. As if three times in amazingly quick succession had not been enough. Each time she had grown bolder, more uninhibited, more playful, more a woman than any he had ever known.

Tenderly, he pulled the blanket higher over her naked shoulder. She muttered something, her brow puckered and then her cheek found his chest, and her face relaxed and she went perfectly still. That her trust in him crossed over the barrier between waking and sleeping touched him in yet another way.

It was getting light outside the window.

He contemplated the gift she had given him, stroked her hair, and her cheek, before finally lying down beside her, pulling her into him, wrapping his arms protectively around her. She wriggled close in her sleep, sighed against him.

After all these weeks of feeling so confused, Blake Fallon knew exactly what he wanted.

He wanted to marry her.

That easy.

He wanted to be with her every night, and wake up with her every morning. He wanted to read newspapers in bed with her, and make her tea, and listen to her voice, and feel her eyes on him.

He wanted to make her blush, and make her laugh, and make her lose control over and over again.

He wanted to walk beaches with her, and ride motorcycles, and look at stars. He wanted to see the world through her eyes. He knew it would be a place brand-new to him, exhilarating, full of undiscovered wonders.

He wanted them to run this ranch together. Not him as the boss and her as the secretary, but the two of them as a team.

He realized, ever since she had first come, they had moved more and more in that direction without him realizing it. A team. He thought of her gentle way with the kids, her quick intelligence, her sense of humor, and he felt what she had felt earlier.

As if it was too much emotion, and it would overflow from him.

And the largest emotion was gratitude. That somehow, when he did not in the least deserve it, she had become his.

She was a woman a man could count on. Could relate to. Could lower his defenses with. She was a woman who allowed a man to be completely and utterly himself, and who did not flinch from what that meant.

No, embraced what it meant.

He was suddenly and humbly so grateful for all the days of her life that she had believed herself to be plain and had dressed the part, acted the part.

It might have been the very thing that saved her treasure for him. And now he would have the great privilege of coaxing her beauty out of her day by day, until she believed it. Radiated it. Was it.

He could picture them growing old together, which startled him. He had never ever looked at a woman and thought of her in terms of the future. Heaven forbid he should think about her hair turning white, and wrinkles appearing around her eyes. None of the women he dated would have much appreciated that projection either.

But with Holly it was a delightful picture. She was one of those women who truly would become better as she aged. She was like a fall-blooming flower, that hardy breed that put the bright blossoms of spring to shame. Fall flowers had strength and resilience, a depth that showed itself in the color that shone forth long after so much else had faded.

Holly Lamb possessed a beauty that went beyond the astonishing hazel shades of her eyes. She possessed a loveliness of soul, and he felt so fortunate that he had seen that first about her.

Blake startled himself further by realizing he could picture her pregnant. All the days of his life he had thought he would not have children. He had thought of the bitter days of his own childhood and reached the conclusion he had been left without the skills necessary to raise a child of his own. A child who was happy and healthy, who had enough self-worth to give the world the gift of himself or herself. The years as director of the Hopechest had, oddly, done nothing to change this assessment of himself.

But when he pictured Holly pregnant, her tummy blossoming with his baby within her, and her breasts growing full, he felt an exquisite tenderness, a yearning to one day have a family with her.

He knew why he had never been able to picture himself as a father before.

Because the magic ingredient had been missing.

The ingredient that could turn a man's hard years into his lessons and his gifts. The ingredient that healed the things a man might carry with him and inadvertently use to hurt others.

The ingredient was love.

With love a man who had spent his childhood either running or locked up would be able to put that aside. With love, a man who had never been read to, or held, would know how to hold his own children, how to cuddle close to them and read them bedtime stories. With love, a man who had played pool instead of Little League, could pitch balls to his own son or daughter.

With the love that shone in Holly's eyes, he could be more a man than he had ever hoped or believed before.

Tomorrow he would go and buy a ring.

The choice would be hers.

But he knew what her choice would be. He had seen it in her eyes. He had been looking at that choice in her eyes for a long, long time.

Imagine her being patient enough to wait until he got it.

He knew what her answer would be to his question "Will you marry me?" and he felt peace. Blake Fallon was a man who, for years now, had thought out each of his actions carefully, analytically, practically.

And lost some part of himself in the process.

The part of him that worked on instinct, survived on instinct, gloried in the adventure of the heart.

Tonight he felt returned to that part of himself. That finally his personality, all of it, could dwell within his own body in peace, integrated.

The wild part of him wanted her, now and forever.

The respectable part of him knew that meant marrying her.

But he let the wild side have the last word: soon. He would marry her with great haste. For her. So that she would never feel a moment's guilt about what had transpired between them. Or a moment's anxiety that it would not last, that it was a flash in the pan.

He would marry her with great haste. For him. To honor that voice within him that he had silenced for too long, that told him exactly what he needed to survive. More, it told him what he needed to be happy.

He needed Holly Lamb.

He needed her like air and water and sunshine. His soul needed her.

He needed her in order that he become the man he was meant to be. Not just a respected man, not just a man who had risen above the troubles of his youth, not just a successful man. But a man who knew how to love. How to give his heart. How to accept love in return. That was the essential element that had been missing from Blake Fallon.

For the first time since the water on the Hopechest Ranch had been poisoned, Blake fell into a deep and untroubled sleep.

That sleep was shattered, after what seemed like only seconds, by a bloodcurdling scream.

Thirteen

The monster was enormous. He had red leathery skin that bubbled briskly like oil boiling. He snorted smoke and his eyes were orange and evil, black-slatted like a snake's. Under each of his warty arms he held a rusty barrel, clearly marked.

DMBE. And in smaller letters DiMethyl Butyl Ether.

Now he was at the wellhead, and the monster peeled the soldered cap off the well with no more effort than it took to peel back the lid off a tin of anchovies. And then he squeezed the barrels in his monster-huge hands, and the bottom and the tops blew off, and liquid began to ooze out, huge dollops of it falling down the well pipe, splashing into the water.

The liquid was luminous, and green. Holly could

tell by looking at it that it held death and destruction, hell and heartbreak.

The monster was laughing now, and she felt startled. Did she know that laughter? Did she recognize it? The laughter was a human sound, not as evil as she might have expected, but hard and cynical, an edge of meanness in it.

A feeling of terror encompassed her. A feeling that she knew the monster.

As if sensing the presence of the dreamer, he turned, looked at her, and his face began to shift, to melt before her eyes.

Always before when the dream had reached this point, Holly had awakened, screaming and terrified, knowing the face below the monster's would be the most horrifying thing she had ever seen.

But tonight, even though she was afraid, she felt oddly safe and warm, protected, as if something much stronger than the monster was holding her in its embrace.

Not breathing, not blinking, Holly waited for the monster to show her his face.

She watched, horrified, fascinated, as the red scales fell away, the lumpy warts disintegrated, bone structure appeared, pink skin, human skin. The monster was a man.

She knew suddenly where she recognized the laughter from.

You're going to work where? For how much? The laughter. *You're crazy. You have the brains to do anything, my girl, anything. Come work for me. Together we could conquer the world, you and I.*

My girl. My girl. My girl.

Something in her began to scream, her denial desperate. No. No. *No. Stop.* She had decided she didn't want to see. She begged the monster to stop. She didn't want to know. But the face kept emerging, taking shape, forming before her eyes.

She tried to turn away before her world collapsed, but there were arms around her. She fought them, but they held, so strong, not allowing her to escape.

She tried to cover her eyes, she tried not to look. She shut her eyes tight.

But even the closed eyes did not help. She knew. And she was not allowed to escape what she knew any longer. She saw the face, and her screams intensified. The monster's face was the most horrifying face she had ever seen.

Not because the man was ugly. No, not that. He wasn't ugly at all. Plain, her mother would have said. *You inherited your looks from your father.*

That was why it was so horrifying. Because she had expected to see the face of a stranger. And instead she found herself looking into a face nearly as familiar to her as her own.

Her father.

Her father was the monster.

"Holly, wake up. Geez, that's quite the right punch. Hey, you're going to give me a black eye. Come out of it. Come on, baby."

Holly jerked awake, stared uncomprehending. Her screams still seemed to hang, chilling, in the bedroom air.

"Blake?" For a moment she was so disoriented she thought she must still be dreaming. Blake in her bed?

"Yeah, Blake. Were you expecting someone else?" He raised a wicked, teasing eyebrow at her.

But the other dream held her in its grip. She tried to shake free of it, but could not. Holly began to tremble, trying to hold back the revulsion and fear she felt. The dream had been trying to tell her for months, and she had been too afraid to face its truth.

Only tonight, in the arms of the man who had shown her a piece of heaven, shared that piece of heaven with her, had she finally felt safe and strong. Safe and strong enough to look into the face of that monster.

"Shhh," he said, "Holly, it was only a dream."

He wrapped his arms tight around her, stroked her hair, murmured against her neck. How wonderful that would have felt, if it was only a dream, to come awake to him.

The tears came, the sobs wracked her body. It wasn't only a dream. She knew that with a terrible certainty.

She knew who had sabotaged the ranch. She had known all along, in some dark corner of her mind. Her father had done it, as coldly, as analytically as he had done everything else in his life.

What was she going to say to Blake?

Oh, God, what if he believed she had seduced him to cover up for her father? What if he thought she had known all along? Here she had been accepting credit for getting the water turned off so quickly.

Hadn't her father called, in the middle of the chaos, to see if she was all right?

He'd called way before the press got hold of the story. Had it been he who suggested the ranch check the water as the source of the illness? But why would he do that, if he had really poisoned the water in the first place?

At the last minute, had he decided to save her?

He'd made it evident ever since she took this job that he felt it was beneath her, a waste of her talent and brains.

How he had scorned her wanting to help the children. Pollyanna. Bleeding Heart. Goody-Two-Shoes. Those were his comments about her.

His comments about the kids had been even more cutting, more cruel. Junior thugs, he'd called the boys from The Shack, eating at the government trough, in between sessions of preying on society. He'd said even worse things about the girls at Emily's House.

She had tried to tell him how she felt, but he had brushed her comments aside. And she really hadn't given what he said another thought. Spouting off was just her dad. He was cynical. And hard. And cold. He had a mean streak.

But was he dangerous?

Surely, for all his faults he could not poison children. His own daughter.

"Holly, come back, sweetheart. Where are you?"

She tried to focus on Blake, as if he would be something solid to hold on to. "The dream," she murmured reluctantly. "I've had the most awful dream."

"The one about the monster poisoning the water? Tell me about it again," he said, his voice so tender, so concerned about her, the voice she had waited her whole life to hear.

"I can't," she whispered.

"Okay, think about something else, then. Look at the sun coming in the windows. It's past nine. Do you want me to cook you breakfast? I make a mean Spanish omelet, and I bet you have all the ingredients."

How she appreciated him trying to bring her back, trying to comfort her. If she was not mistaken, that was a brand-new light shining in his eyes.

Love.

Looking at him, Holly felt as though her heart were breaking into jagged little pieces. The hard, cold truth was she was completely unworthy of him. Because she did not know if she had the courage to do the right thing.

Could she turn in her own father? Could she mention her suspicions to anyone?

Could she not mention her suspicions?

Could she hold them inside and hope Todd had finished whatever he had set out to do? What if he wasn't finished? Would she really wait until he managed to kill somebody before she would do what was right?

What if her silence killed a child?

"Oh, God," she said out loud.

"Holly! It was a dream." His voice so calm, so certain. It was a voice that a woman wanted to wake up to forever.

That had been the dream. The dream had been the night she just had spent with Blake. A night so full of laughter and passion and wondrous discovery. A night she would never forget, that she would hold to and find strength in the days to come. The weeks. The months. Maybe the years. She could not ask Blake to care about her now, she could not accept his caring.

"Blake," she said, "you have to leave now. I have something I have to do today. It's important."

She was amazed by the coolness in her tone.

Blake looked stunned. Then the hurt chased, like clouds, through the clear gray of his eyes. Somehow that was much easier to handle than the tender concern.

"I think we should talk about that nightmare."

"Maybe later," she said, resisting the note of authority in his voice. "Blake, please just go."

He was not the kind of man who would ever beg, she knew that. He got up and found his clothes. He sat on the edge of the bed and slipped his jeans over his legs, stood up, and tugged them over the steel curve of his buttock. They settled snugly around his waist as he did up the snap.

She watched him with the kind of hunger of a woman who was saving memories. How she wanted this to be part of her life. To be able to watch him throw clothes over his magnificent body every day, feel the wanting start in her anew.

Did women grow tired of these little things, like watching their man get dressed in the morning? Did those small things lose their ability to compel, after time?

She could not imagine such a thing. She could not imagine a day would ever come when she would tire of him. His back was still to her, as he pulled the crumpled shirt over the broad surface of his shoulders.

Shoulders she had touched and kissed and *known*.

For some reason, she pictured him growing old. She knew who he would be like. Joe Colton. Handsome and proud and full of vitality.

She knew if she followed these thoughts any further she would begin to cry, and that Blake would turn back to her and return to the bed. He would put his arms around her and tuck her head into his shoulder, and he would not rest until she told him.

Her strength was ebbing as she saw him getting ready to leave. If he gave her one last chance, she would probably tell everything.

She saw him turning back toward her, and she flipped over on her side, as if she did not care if he went.

"Holly?"

"Hmm?" she didn't turn back over.

"You want me to call you later?"

"I think it might be better if I called you."

Silence, and then the door whispered open, and she heard his feet pad across her floor, imagined him stopping to put on his boots, glancing back at her bedroom door one last time. And then she heard the outside door open and close quietly.

It sounded terribly final.

And then she began to weep.

But there was no time for weeping. There was a madman out there, and children in danger, and she needed to know what she was going to do about it.

She realized she had no choice. That was why she had not dared to look at the face in her dream until she had found a safe place, a place that had made her more than she ever was before. A woman of courage, who took chances.

She had no choice, but whichever way she turned now her life would be changed forever, tinged with the faint ugliness of a woman who had betrayed her own father.

Or the worse ugliness of a woman who had betrayed the trust of the children in her care. Not to mention the man who had given his heart to her last night.

Sick with grief and trepidation, she went to the phone book and fumbled through it until she found the number she was looking for.

A woman answered the phone.

For some reason she sounded like the woman that Holly might have been this morning if she had not had that dream.

She sounded like a woman who was happy, in love, satiated.

Holly was shocked at herself for drawing that kind of conclusion about a woman she barely knew.

"Libby, it's Holly Lamb. I need to talk to Rafe, if he's there."

He came to the phone. His voice was deep and strong. Reassuring. It was the voice of a man a woman could believe in.

And, Holly hoped, trust her fate to.

"Rafe, it's Holly Lamb. I need to see you," she said. "It's very urgent. No, don't come here." Blake would have too many questions to ask if Rafe showed up at her cabin. "I'll come to you. In an hour? Fine." She wrote down the instructions he gave her to find his home on the reservation, took a deep breath, and wiped the tears from her eyes. She looked like hell, and it just didn't seem to matter at all anymore what she looked like.

The roads, thankfully, were uncrowded, because Holly drove terribly, her mind so racked with confusion.

Rafe answered the door and invited her in. She followed him back to the kitchen, wrapped her hand around the coffee cup he set in front of her.

She could tell, he was taking her measure, and accurately.

She knew why he and Blake were good friends. He was physically big and strong, like Blake, but it was more. Holly could feel the quiet strength running through him.

He didn't push her, just sipped his own coffee and watched her.

"Blake told me you have a primary suspect in the water poisoning," she finally said. "And that you wouldn't tell him who it was."

She could tell she shocked him. Whatever he had been expecting, it wasn't this. And her knowledge that the suspect was her father was confirmed by the hood that dropped warily over his eyes.

"Did he send you here to ask me who it was?" he

asked, after a moment, "because if I didn't tell him, I won't tell you."

"You don't have to tell me," she said quietly. "I know."

He stared at her, and she could tell again she had taken him by surprise, and that he was not a man used to being surprised.

"You know?" he repeated, quietly.

"I know." She fought to keep the quiver from her voice and succeeded. "I know that my father poisoned the water."

Rafe took a sip of his coffee, eyed her warily.

"So, are you here on his behalf?" He gave away nothing, neither confirming or denying her father was a suspect.

"On behalf of my father?" she asked incredulously. "What age are you from? I am not here because a man sent me here. I am here because I can't live with myself if I don't do something about what I know."

"How long have you thought it was your father?"

"Since this morning," she said, and then gave in to the feeling she could trust him. She told him about the dreams, about finally this morning the monster having a face. She did not mention the reason the monster's face had become clear to her this morning—because Blake was with her.

"Holly, a dream? That's not exactly cold, hard fact. It's hardly admissible in a court of law."

"You know it's him, don't you?" she pressed.

Rafe ran an uneasy hand through his hair.

"What are you going to do about it?" she asked softly. "He's still free."

She saw in his eyes that he had crossed some line and had decided to trust her as much as she was already trusting him.

"We don't have enough evidence to make an arrest. No traces of the substance in his car, no witnesses, no motive."

"You don't have anything."

He sighed. "Except that hunch. The one that's never wrong."

"I think I could get him to confess to me. I could tape it."

Rafe stared at her, and hope leapt in his dark eyes, before he savagely doused it. "No."

"Why not?"

"Look, you've seen too many cop shows. Things go very wrong on operations like that, and that's with trained people doing the dance."

"You're thinking something else," she deduced.

He shot her a look. "Smart girl."

"And?"

"Okay. Blake would kill me. How's that?"

She allowed herself to feel a small thrill of joy that Blake must have confided in his friend that he had feelings for her. Last night hadn't been an impulse on his part, it had been a culmination.

She forced herself not to think that now. She had to stay strong and clear.

She sensed she still did not have the whole story. "There's something else."

Rafe sighed. "A man was sent here from the Environmental Protection Agency. His name was Charlie O'Connell. He died in a single-vehicle car accident. The circumstances are suspicious.''

She felt the blood drain from her face. ''You think my father killed him?''

He shrugged. ''It's a possibility that makes me not very inclined to ask you to get a confession out of him.''

Why did she feel so newly shocked? Why was this any worse than what he had already done? The fact that people had not died from the contaminated water seemed to be more by accident than design.

If anything, the suspicion of murder should be hardening her resolve. Her father was a dangerous man. And she might be the only person he would ever admit that to.

She leaned across the table, drilled Rafe with her eyes. ''Mr. James, I am getting that confession from my father. On tape. I'm doing it with or without your help. So you decide which it's going to be.''

''Look, you're not getting involved in this.''

''I'm already involved in this.'' She stood up. ''Fine. I can go buy one of those pocket-size tape recorders and hide it and go see my father. I don't need your help.''

He sat there, and she could tell he was debating whether to call her bluff. Only she wasn't bluffing. She took a step toward the door.

''Wait.''

She turned back toward him. ''Yes?''

Rafe looked at her grimly, and then a reluctant smile played across his firm lips. ''No wonder he's

crazy about you,'' he said. ''Has he told you that
yet?''

''Yes,'' she said, but she would not let the confusion of that yes weaken her, change her mind, make
her thinking less clear. She had to get this out of the
way before she could give Blake one more thought.

If she did not look after this, their relationship was
doomed.

And maybe it was anyway.

''I'm going to give Rory Sinclair a call and ask
him over. I'd like his take on this, his input. Is that
all right with you?''

She nodded.

It seemed like only a few minutes before Rory was
at the door. Rory had been to the Hopechest office
before, and it was just as evident why he and Blake
were friends as it was evident why Rafe and Blake
were friends.

The three men had something the same about
them—that easy self-assurance of men who knew
who they were and what they were about. The easy
confidence of strong men who had relied on their
strength and won because of it.

When Rory joined them at the kitchen table, Rafe
encouraged her to tell it again.

She repeated how the dream had revealed the truth
to her.

Rory shot Rafe a look that said *So what? We can't
use it in court.*

''Tell him the rest,'' Rafe said grimly.

''I'm going to tape a confession from my father.''

"What?" Rory exploded. "You sure the hell are not."

"Yes, I am."

"She said she's doing it with or without our help," Rafe said.

Rory gave her a stern look. "It's too dangerous. Miss Lamb—Holly—I don't think you know what you're playing with here. You're thinking of him as Daddy, but he has willfully harmed a lot of people." Rory cast Rafe a glance.

"I told her our suspicions about O'Connell."

"So, you know your father may have even killed a man. You don't just go marching into something like that and say fess up, and think he will."

"Give me credit for having a few brains," she said coldly, "and for knowing my father. I believe I know exactly how to play to him."

"I think she can pull it off," Rafe said reluctantly.

Rory rocked his chair up on its back legs and looked from Rafe to her and back again. "I'll call Kane Lummus," he said, and got up and did so. "He's on his way. Blake is going to kill us."

"My thoughts exactly," Rafe said glumly.

"Blake doesn't even have to know about it," she said evenly.

"Right."

"Sure."

"He doesn't!"

"He'll know," Rafe told her sharply.

"How?"

"You don't know Blake like I do. The man runs on instinct. He follows his gut. He'll know something's up and he won't rest until he knows what it is. Especially if it involves you.''

It was the second time Rafe had implied Blake had been harboring feelings for her longer than she might have guessed.

Possibly as long as she had been harboring them for him?

All of them froze as they heard the deep rumble of a motorcycle engine outside the house. Rory and Rafe exchanged glances as the engine shut down.

A moment later, Blake was leaning against the kitchen door, his helmet swinging in his hand, his black leather jacket undone. He regarded the three of them solemnly.

''Do you mind telling me what's going on here?''

Fourteen

Nobody looked very happy to see him, Blake noted. And that went double for Holly. She was exchanging looks with *his* friends that begged them not to tell.

Tell what?

Angry and confused after leaving Holly this morning, he had gone home and done the mature thing. The masculine thing. He had sulked and licked his wounds. And sulked some more. Somehow, being asked to leave was not what he had pictured for his first morning as a man in love.

Then he had heard her car start up and gotten to his bedroom window just in time to see her pulling away.

Apparently she wasn't sulking. She was getting on with her *important* plans, just as she had said she was going to.

He'd decided to get on his motorbike and head for the coast. The truth was it was a variation on sulking where he entertained various notions, including that of never coming back. But he hadn't gone very far before memories of the night before came back to torment him.

Last night had been a night of breathtaking magnificence. It wouldn't be stretching it to say being with Holly was hands down the best experience of his entire life. And he had *known* it was the same for her, with that wonderful feeling of knowing that came from being with Holly. He knew her. She knew him.

How had it all blown up?

The nightmare. Whatever she had dreamed had gripped her so strong he could not break it. He remembered they had discussed her dream before. A silly dream, the subconscious dealing with all her fears surrounding the ranch's water.

In her dream a monster poisoned the ranch water. But when she had awoken this morning, she seemed to feel the dream had told her something real. Did she think she knew who had poisoned the water?

Maybe she thought it was him.

The thought was so stunning he had to pull off the road to consider it. The very thought was an affront to his ego, and everything he had come to hope he stood for: decency, integrity, honesty. It seemed impossible the woman he loved could harbor such a notion about him and yet what else could explain that quick turnaround? Holly had gone, it seemed, from loving him madly and completely to not being able to get rid of him fast enough.

Did Holly think he'd poisoned the water? Could he give his love to a woman who could believe such a despicable thing of him?

Well, why not him? He came from a bad gene pool. Good old Dad had managed to wreck Joe Colton's birthday party with a gun. And maybe Blake wasn't so far removed from his own bad-boy days to have truly outrun the stigma.

Or maybe she had the thought he had been nursing: What if the poisoned water was an act of revenge? One of Joe Colton's many admirers doing payback for Blake's father's attempt on Joe's life?

None of his conjecture rang true.

But if it was true, at the very least he could find out who had really done it. If he knew that, maybe he could help her put a stop to those nightmares that had such a hold on her she thought they were real.

Even if it didn't bring her back to him. Maybe love didn't do that. Maybe love didn't ask for anything in return.

Rafe knew.

And if he had to, Blake was prepared to choke it out of him.

His astonishment at seeing that Holly had beat him to Rafe's was nearly enough to make him turn around, go home and sulk some more.

But then he recognized Rory's vehicle was there, too.

It seemed so out of kilter that three of the people he cared about most in the world were sharing something without him, that not even his pride could make him turn around and mind his own business.

What if she had brought her suspicions to them?

If she had, it would be better to face it now, turn it around now, before it was too late, than to go home and stew about all the different possibilities that might be unfolding in that house.

Hell, maybe she was even planning a surprise party for him.

The momentary warmth and relief that thought brought to him disappeared as soon as he saw their faces. These were not three people planning a surprise party.

"Do you mind telling me what's going on here?" he repeated, not missing the guilty looks that were passing between Rafe and Rory.

Nobody said anything.

"Do you think I did it?" he asked quietly. He was looking at all of them, or pretending to. Really, he was only looking at her.

And her stunned look told him he was way off the mark.

"Did what?" Rory asked him, genuinely incredulous.

Rafe shook his head, looked from Blake to Holly, and got it. Of course. "Never mind," he told Rory, "the man's not thinking straight."

"Well, maybe you could help me out then," Blake suggested, the silkiness of his tone not masking the threat in the least.

Rafe sighed, sent Holly an apologetic look. "It's Todd Lamb."

Holly lowered her head, looked at the hands folded in her lap. Her face was white with pain—and shame.

"Todd Lamb what?" he asked. Dead? Maimed? Ill? And then, sickeningly, he knew. They didn't think Blake had poisoned the ranch's water. They thought it was Holly's father.

Blake went to Holly, slid back the empty chair beside her. He sat down and pried one hand out of her lap and held it tight. He wanted to rake her over the coals for not telling him, for not trusting him, but he felt like a fool.

Rafe had practically told him who it was. Had told him Holly was going to need him to get through it. Why hadn't he figured it out? Her father was behind the contaminated water.

Rafe was right. Blake hadn't figured it out because he wasn't thinking straight. He hadn't been thinking straight for a long time. For as long as he had loved Holly. When had he started loving her? The first time he'd seen her on the sofa with a little kid on her lap instead of at her desk? Or when she'd started framing those pictures? Or the first time he'd heard her laugh? Or was it after that first real conversation they'd had, and it had gone deep and true?

When had he first known it?

That was easy. When Tomas had told him he'd held a knife to her throat, even though Blake had been able to go on denying it for a while longer.

"So," he said, squeezing her hand, trying to tell her it was all right, "what's next?"

The discomfort grew in the room.

Rory spoke. "We're waiting for Kade to get here. Holly's going to wear a wire," he finally said. "She's going to tape a confession."

Blake stared at his two oldest friends. Well, apparently they weren't thinking straight, either.

"Not in my lifetime," he told them quietly.

Rafe shot Holly a look. "Yeah, well, that's kind of what we said, too."

"Good, we're all in agreement."

Holly pulled her hand free from his with amazing strength, and looked at him, the shame gone from her eyes. They were snapping green fire.

"*We're* all in agreement? I don't think so."

"Huh?"

"I'll tell you the same thing I told them. I'm going to tape a confession from him—with or without their help. Or yours."

"Like hell you are."

"I'm not asking your permission."

Blake had the very naughty thought that he couldn't wait to see this side of her personality in bed. The tigress had surprised him. She had really been keeping it a secret that she was part hellcat.

Then, he reminded himself grimly, his sharing a bed with her again was somewhat contingent on her not getting herself killed.

"What are you thinking?" he asked her. "It sounds like a script from a bad movie."

She glared at him and folded her arms over her chest in a way that did not bode well for his veto power.

He tried a different tone of voice. Patient. Wise. "What you're proposing sounds foolishly dangerous."

It didn't seem to convince her.

"It's foolishly dangerous to leave my father running loose. That's what I'm thinking. What's to stop him from repeating his crime? Which of the kids are you willing to sacrifice so I'll be safe forever? One of them? All of them?"

"Look, these two are both law enforcement professionals. I'm sure they have a plan to nab your father that doesn't put you in such grave personal danger. Don't you? Rory? Rafe?"

His friends looked at him silently.

Rafe finally spoke. "He hasn't left a trail, Blake. All we've got right now is a fistful of suspicions and a hunch. The truth is he'd probably have to act again before we got him."

Act again. Blake felt sick.

"You should probably know we suspect him in the death of Charles O'Connell, as well," Rory said bleakly.

Blake let go of a trail of expletives, intended to convey his displeasure to Holly in no uncertain terms. After which she was supposed to back down.

"I have to do it," she told him. "Do you understand?"

He took a deep breath and looked into her eyes. He saw the strength there, the absolute courage to back up her convictions. Unfortunately he did understand. And unfortunately, he thought a lot of her having to do this was about her loving him.

Having to prove herself to him, the same way Blake had felt driven to prove himself to Joe Colton after he'd been rescued from a life of crime, and then again after his own father had tried to kill Joe.

He understood those demons. And he knew he could not make them go away for her.

Even so, he said, "Don't do this for me, Holly. You don't have to prove anything to me."

"I'm doing it for myself."

He nodded, defeated, and then taking a deep breath, he committed to the path the other three of them were already on. If he couldn't stop her, he had to protect her.

"I'm in," he said. "Tell me what you want me to do."

And so they spent agonizing hours coming up with a plan, rehearsing Holly over and over again so that she wouldn't slip up.

Kade Lummus arrived, a man who inspired confidence. He had several other members of the Prosperino Police Department with him.

Two things became apparent to Blake. The first was that she probably could get her father to confess. She knew him. She knew the exact combination of ego-stroking and admiration to use. But the second thing was the frightening one: There were too many things that could go wrong, too many variables they could not even begin to speculate about sitting here in the safety of Rafe's kitchen, slugging back pot after pot of black coffee.

Libby slipped in unobtrusively and kept refurbishing the coffee. Just as unobtrusively, she provided sandwiches and snacks.

Despite his anxiety, Blake couldn't help but notice how well Libby and Rafe read each other's signs. He thought it was one woman in a million who would prepare coffee and disappear like that, not allowing her curiosity about what was happening in that tension-rife kitchen to get the better of her.

By the end of that long afternoon, pieces were falling into place. Bumper beepers had been delivered. One had been installed on Holly's car. The other would be attached to the bumper of Todd's car as soon as darkness fell. The tape recorder arrived. And then a surveillance van.

Blake wouldn't let anybody else touch her. Kade told him what to do. He taped the small recorder to her tiny midriff, trying not to let the touch of her skin drive him wild with remembered passion that only fueled his fear for her.

Libby, a few sizes larger than Holly, lent her an oversize sweater. The recorder had to be turned on only once, after that it was voice activated. Rafe had her practice over and over again, until she could clear her throat and touch the on button seamlessly, every single time.

Darkness fell.

Without a word, Rory took the bumper beeper and left.

Blake prayed that Lamb's car would be gone, that he would have other business tonight, or that he parked his car where it would be too risky for Rory to crawl underneath it and attach the beeper to the bumper.

But Rory was back within half an hour. Again, he didn't say a word. Only nodded.

Taking a deep breath, Holly picked up the phone.

Rafe grabbed it from her and pressed the code to

block the number, just in case her father had caller ID. He handed it back to her, and she dialed her father's number, then put it on the speaker.

Again, Blake found himself praying. Don't let him be home. If he's home, let him not answer.

But on the third ring, Lamb picked up.

"Hi, Dad, it's Holly."

"I don't think I know anybody by that name."

It was a joke, of sorts, but Blake saw Holly flinch from the casual cruelty of it.

"Your daughter?" she said.

A short laugh. "I know. It's just I haven't heard from you for so long, I didn't remember I had a daughter."

Tell him the phone works two ways, Blake thought savagely, and then realized Holly was much better at this than he. Because she remembered the point wasn't to get Todd's back up.

"The crisis at the ranch just kept me really busy for a while," Holly said. "But I'd love to make it up to you. Do you want to go for dinner tonight?"

Hesitation. Just enough, Blake thought angrily, to make her know he had to debate between a night of watching baseball on television or spending time with her.

"I guess we could do that," Todd said.

There was a collective but silent sigh in the kitchen.

"The Red Herring?" Holly said. "I've heard it's good."

"By Prosperino's standards or the rest of the world's?"

A man who found fault with everything.

"I just heard it was good."

"All right. You want me to pick you up?"

Three men shook their heads violently. If they could keep Holly and her father out of vehicles and in public, that would be safer. The bumper beepers were a backup they were all praying they wouldn't have to use.

Rory had already arranged for them to have a quiet corner in the restaurant, completely private, in case Todd accepted the invitation.

Their waiter was going to be an FBI agent.

"Oh, no," Holly said, "there's no sense coming all the way out here. I'll meet you." She glanced at the clock. "Say around six-thirty."

"All right, doll. I just thought I'd save you some gas money. The way you get paid at that miserable job, I'm surprised you can afford to drive."

"That's one of the things I want to talk to you about."

"I hope this means you've come to your senses."

"I'll see you at dinner, Daddy."

"Right-o."

She hung up the phone.

Rory said it all. He shook his head. "Charming, isn't he? Sorry, Holly."

Rafe looked at his watch. "Thirty minutes. Let's go over it one more time."

And they settled in to work.

"I need a few minutes alone with Holly before she goes," Blake said, as the minutes ticked down.

Rafe and Rory left the room.

"You still have time to back out," he told her quietly. He could see she was afraid and at war with herself. Well, he of all people in the world knew what it was to put away any final illusions you had about a parent.

"I'm not backing out," she said stubbornly.

"I wish you would have told me about the dream this morning."

She looked at her hands. "Blake, please believe this. It wasn't because I didn't care for you. It was because—" Her voice faltered. "It was just because."

He crossed the distance between them and swept her into his arms, covered her lips with his own. Not to convince her not to go, but so that she could carry it within her, like a shield to protect her.

His love.

Had he ever said the words before? Maybe many years ago, to his mother. Until he had admitted she was deaf to the words.

He felt afraid of saying them now.

And yet he knew he had to overcome that fear. That she needed to hear the words, and that he needed to say them.

"Holly, I love you."

Her eyes went very wide, and her mouth dropped open.

"Are you just saying that?" she asked.

He smiled. "Those aren't words a man just says."

She smiled then, radiant, before a different look passed over her face, a look of intense doubt.

He wanted to erase it by asking her to marry him now, but would that make her unable to focus on the job that needed to be done? Better to wait than to take that chance.

There was a soft rap on the door, and Rory put his head in. "Show time."

Blake felt her tremble against him, and then she took a deep breath and stepped back. He looked at her and added courage to the list of attributes he most loved about her.

He didn't want to let her go. But he knew if he tried to hold her now it would change something between them that could never be repaired.

Love could never be allowed to diminish what your beloved was. It had to be the force that made them more than they had been before. Greater. Fully themselves.

Holly was a woman of integrity and honor and courage. If he loved her, he could not be the one to ask her not to be those things.

So, though he wanted to hold her to him forever, instead he kissed her on the tip of her nose.

"I'll be right outside in the surveillance van," he told her. "I'll be there for you."

She smiled bravely. "Knowing that makes it so much easier."

He wished she would say the words he most needed to hear. What if she never came back and she had not told him she loved him? He could not allow himself to think that.

He let her go.

She whirled from him, shoulders back and chin up, and walked out of the room. She accepted some last-minute instructions from Rory, and then went and got in her car.

The three men got in the van that had been delivered. Blake was impressed with it. On the outside it was unobtrusive. An old gray panel van that said Walt's Plumbing on the side of it. It looked like it hadn't been through a car wash in a long time.

All the men were silent and tense. Rafe took the driver's seat, Blake and Rory went into the back.

It was incredibly high tech. Rory slipped on a pair of headphones and turned on a computer.

"Her beeper working?" Blake asked.

Rory gave him a look. "You think I'd wait until now to find out?"

"Sorry," Blake muttered.

Rory handed him a set of headphones. "Last-minute instructions. This is Rafe's and my gig. You are here for the ride. No heroics. This is not Hollywood."

Blake scowled at him. "You don't need to tell me this isn't Hollywood. My gut told me a few hours ago. A bucket of popcorn never made it feel like this."

"You love her?" Rory asked, not looking at him, but fiddling with something on the computer monitor.

"Yeah," Blake growled.

"That just complicates everything. Because I know if it was Peggy going in there I'd be a wreck. And I'd make mistakes. So you leave the thinking to Rafe and me, you got it?"

"Yeah," Blake muttered insincerely. As if, if he

felt her life was in danger, he was just going to sit there and let them call the shots.

Rory must have seen the look on his face, because he sighed and shook his head.

''She's at the restaurant,'' he said, showing Blake the map that had come up on his computer screen.

Rafe parked about half a block from the restaurant, away from the street lamps. ''I'll do visual,'' he said quietly.

Rory nodded.

The time ticked by with excruciating slowness.

''There's Todd,'' Rafe said.

Blake felt his skin prickling. He had to fight down the urge to leap out of the van and go take care of this himself.

Rory touched his sleeve and gave him a warning look.

They waited for the tape to turn on. There were several tense minutes of disconnection, and then with a click a tape recorder in the van turned on, the reels began to slowly turn, and Blake heard her voice, strong and clear. He marveled at her light tone. One thing he wouldn't have thought she could do was act.

She was so damned genuine.

They chatted for a few minutes about her mother and another mutual friend, and then she brought the conversation around.

''So, Daddy, how do you like being vice president of Springer?''

''It's a start,'' he said.

''A start?'' she said with just the right touch of admiration.

Todd was happy to fill her in on where he was going next. Right to the top. Had his eye on the president's chair.

He was a man who loved talking about himself. He hadn't asked Holly one question about her life, had not shown the least bit of interest in her. He ordered for her, without consulting her.

He had nearly put Blake to sleep, when Holly stepped up the heat.

"So, Daddy, now that David Corbett has been cleared, have you any thoughts on how the water at the ranch got poisoned?"

"I think it was just an accident," he said, and the men listening could hear the caution in his voice.

"An accident?" she asked. "Really? How could a restricted chemical get in the water by accident?"

"Aquifers change, maps become outdated. A little earth tremor can do it."

"I don't understand," she said.

"I don't think whoever poisoned the water ever meant to hurt anyone at the ranch, Holly."

"Really?"

To the men listening in she was playing the interested schoolgirl to the hilt.

Todd lowered his voice. "Springer has been looking to expand operations. Contaminated water drives down land prices."

"Careful, Holly," Rory said in an undertone.

"Springer has lots of money," she said. "Why would they care about land prices?"

"*They* don't. If somebody else cheaply picked up

the land, or a lease on the land, they could sell it to Springer at a major profit.''

''Wow,'' Holly breathed, ''that's brilliant, isn't it?''

''Just guessing, of course,'' Todd said.

''Well, it makes sense. It has to be an insider at Springer. Someone who knows they want to expand and has access to that chemical.''

''We're conducting an internal investigation.''

''But whoever did this is way too smart to get caught, aren't they?''

''That would be my guess.''

Both men listening caught the sickening note of pride in the voice.

''How much money would you think would be involved in something like that?''

''Millions,'' Todd said.

''She's walking him right into it,'' Rory said with satisfaction. ''He trusts her.''

''Did I tell you my do-gooder days are over, Dad?''

''Really? It's about time. I've got a job waiting for you at Springer.''

''Millions sounds more appealing to me.''

Todd was silent, and the men in the van waited to see if she had overplayed her hand.

''What are you saying?'' Todd finally asked, sounding a little nervous.

She lowered her voice. ''I know you did it, Dad. I know it's not over. And I want in.''

Fifteen

Her father cast his eyes around the room nervously. "Be careful what you say."

"Nobody's listening to us." Holly didn't quite know how she pulled that off when the only reason she was staying so calm—almost detached from her own body—was that she knew Blake was listening and she could feel his presence close to her.

It was that, more than the fact that she knew their waiter was an FBI agent, that made her feel safe.

"You never know that for sure," Todd said, fishing in his wallet for some bills, which he threw onto the table.

For a split second she thought she'd overdone it, and he was leaving without her.

"Come on. We'll go for a drive."

"Sure. I didn't feel like dessert anyway." He

wanted to tell her everything. She could tell. Carrying secrets of the magnitude he was carrying weighed a man down, made him feel lonely. Holly sensed his eagerness to unburden himself.

They left the restaurant and she waited while he unlocked the car door and opened it for her. Save for one brief glance at the van when she had come out the door, she forced herself not to look there.

As far as she could tell, Todd hadn't even noticed it.

"Where are we going?" she asked.

"Just for a drive."

She decided to wait him out, to play on her hunch that he wanted to talk. She was right.

"So, doll, what makes you think your old man has been up to no good?"

She realized she needed to get him to do the talking. She needed his confession, not to fill up the tape with her conjecture.

"Who said anything about no good?" she said with a laugh.

"Lots of those little ankle nippers you've been working around got sick."

"Nobody died."

"That's what I thought. Plus, I gave the ranch the Pathfinder. About as close to an apology as could be expected under the circumstances. What more can a man do? So, you think I need a partner?"

"It's going to look mighty suspicious if you obtain that land in your name."

He shot her a look. "I always knew you were a bright girl."

"And not much better if we acquire it in my name."

"So?"

"I've got a friend. We can use her name without getting her involved. She's dumb as a brick. She won't catch on."

"That's my girl."

She realized he didn't know her at all. She would never call one of her friends stupid. He'd never known her, and now he never would. But Holly did not have the luxury of feeling sad about that right now.

"So, tell me everything." They were pulling out of Prosperino and heading toward the coast. Todd turned off on an unmarked road, but he seemed confident of his whereabouts.

She slid a look to the passenger side mirror and felt her heart fall at the absolute blackness behind them. And then she caught the quick flicker of lights and relaxed slightly.

Todd confessed. But she had been wrong about one thing. It was not the burden of his secrets that made him so eager to talk, it was that so far what he considered his brilliance had gone unapplauded, unapproved.

He told all. She was stunned to learn her father had kidnapped Libby Corbett, and she tried not to think of Rafe listening.

"Of course," he said finally, "every plot has a mistake."

She noticed he avoided using the word *crime*.

"You made a mistake?"

"Two of them. I wanted the land on the Crooked Arrow Reservation. When they drilled the new well there, I saw my opportunity. Reserves aren't usually that open to letting go of land, not even lease agreements. Especially since what Springer needs is a test ground for some fairly serious chemicals. Nobody wants that in their backyard. The option is going to a third-world country, but they're always so damned unstable.

"The new well meant they were soon going to be putting houses in the area I wanted. So, they drill a well, I put in a chemical, they test it, and voila, decide it's not safe for people to live there.

"My thinking was if the land had been rendered useless for habitation, I could pick it up or lease it for a song, then sell it or lease it back to Springer for a fortune."

"I did my homework, checked the lay of the land, which was harder than you might think. The aquifer—the water table—had been mapped twelve years ago, but the map was no longer available. I had to track it down, which was the mistake that nearly got me caught, but I'll get to that in a minute.

"Anyway, I went to the state archives and looked at the damned maps, then based on them did the dirty deed. Was it my fault that the map missed a shift under the ground and didn't show that the water would eventually trickle down into the aquifer used by the Hopechest Ranch?"

"Tell me how you nearly got caught," she said, pretending breathless interest in his tale. She was trying to watch the road, which was twisting dangerously now as it hugged the cliffs. It was deeply rutted and didn't seem to ever be used. If anybody was following them, they had long since turned off their headlights.

"The EPA sent a guy out. Charlie O'Connell." He pulled the car over, stopped it, turned off the lights. "Get out. I want to show you something."

She got out her car door and went and stood beside him. He was staring over the edge of the cliff, a look on his face that made her shiver with suppressed terror. She tossed her hair over her shoulder as an excuse to glance back at the road. Nothing.

"I killed a man here," he said softly. "The only one who knew. He got too greedy."

Was it a warning to her?

"You killed somebody?" she stammered, as if this came as a complete surprise to her.

He turned and faced her. "That's what you've got to be prepared to do to get what you want. Anything."

He seemed to be waiting for a reply. She had none.

"He was a useless moron anyway. Government employee, parasite on society. He signed into the state archives to look at those maps, same as me. And guess what? There was my mistake. My name on the sign-in sheet.

"From that, he figured it out. He made a mistake when he thought he was going to be a parasite on me, though. He was feeling sorry for himself because he'd been passed over for promotion once too often. He figured I'd make a pretty good retirement plan, so he tried to blackmail me.

"I played along, even paid him once to lull him into a sense of security. Boy, I'm an actor."

Holly tried not to show her revulsion at this almost gleeful retelling of the tale.

"Told him I was scared to death to get caught paying him. Talked him into meeting me way up here. I waited right over there for him, in one of the company trucks. When he parked, I just drove up behind him and pushed him off."

Holly followed Todd's gaze down the unforgiving cliff.

"I was worried. I'd heard that the exact model and make of a vehicle can be traced from paint, and I knew there was going to be a bit of paint on that bumper. So you know what I did, sweetheart?"

"No," she said in a small voice. He was tickled by all this. It wasn't a man's life to him, people's lives, it was just a big, entertaining game that pitted his craft and cunning against the world.

"I took that vehicle in and parked it in the company garage. And then I suggested we donate it to the Hopechest Ranch. But I thought maybe we should repaint it first, since Springer has all their vehicles custom-painted white. We decided on silver.

"That will teach him to take advantage of me," Todd said, still staring over the cliff. The moon came out from behind a cloud and glanced off his face.

She saw the madness in his eyes.

Had she made the same mistake as that poor EPA man? Had she taken exactly the wrong tact to win her father's confidence? Had he brought her here to kill her? Where was her backup? She had to trust that they were good. She had to trust they were close by, and so good at what they were doing that even though she knew they were there, she could not detect them. Her father, lost in his reverie, didn't have a clue.

She forced confidence into her voice, "So is that why you brought me here? To kill me, too?"

"Holly! How could you think such a thing? Kill my own daughter?"

She saw this was a variation of the honor-among-thieves philosophy. He had his lines he would not cross. Unless of course he discovered the tape recorder strapped to her waist.

"So what's our next step?" she asked, putting careful emphasis on the *our*, trying to get him to think of her as part of his team.

"I don't know yet," he said thoughtfully. "A man like me doesn't ever see failure, only new opportunity. I have two options now. I bet if someone made an offer on the Hopechest Ranch right now, it would go pretty cheap. Or if traces of DMBE started showing up in the water again, that would probably clinch the deal.

"Or I can try again for the reservation with a different wellhead. I skimmed a bit of DMBE from some of the barrels. Put it away for a rainy day." He chuckled softly, as if that was a joke.

"Where is it?"

He tore his gaze away from the cliff, and looked at her. Really looked at her for the first time that night.

His expression became puzzled, wary.

His confession made, Todd seemed to suddenly realize how vulnerable he had made himself.

"So what's with the big turnaround?" he asked, slowly. "Last time I saw you, you were giving Mother Teresa a run for her money. Come to think of it, you even look different. I thought you loved that dead-end job and those good-for-nothing kids."

She didn't like the way he was looking at her, the intensity of his gaze, the sudden hardness in his eyes. She somehow knew if she lied now, she would be in big trouble.

And so, she opted for the truth. The absolute truth.

"I fell in love with my boss."

Her father snickered. "Well, Holly, you aren't really the type to inspire grand passions. Not like your mother."

"I just wanted him to love me the way I loved him."

"Consider yourself lucky he didn't. He probably would have taken advantage of your romantic nature, bedded you a few times and then dumped you in the discard pile. That's the nature of the beast. Even a goody-goody beast like the young Fallon."

With effort, she held her temper, kept her expression bland.

Todd couldn't seem to stop talking now that he had started. "I don't care what people say about his old man. I get tired of the 'Joe Colton, America's Greatest Hero' song that everybody in this valley sings so loud. I was happy when old Emmett took a shot at him. Too bad he missed."

Holly tried to stifle her gasp.

"We could probably get rid of your SOB of a boss if we played our cards right. DMBE is pretty versatile stuff. It's colorless, tasteless, odorless. You could put some in his coffee."

It was more than she could pretend. The gasp escaped her.

"You're in now, Holly girl. You know all my secrets. It's too late to decide you don't have the stomach for it."

She tried to smile, but she could see the strange gleam in his eye, and knew that her father had crossed that fine line between sane and insane at some point that they had all missed. They had missed it because he was clever, and because he never let anyone get too close to him.

Only he was watching her narrowly now, suspiciously. "You're having me on, aren't you?" he asked softly, understanding dawning in his eyes.

"What do you mean?" she asked, backing away from him as he moved closer.

"You couldn't kill anybody. You couldn't poison the water system. I can see that in your eyes. You used to blubber if I swatted a fly when you were a kid."

She said nothing.

"Now you've gone and put me in a really bad position. You know everything, but you don't really want to be my partner. I'm getting a little nervous here, Holly."

"You're reading it wrong," she said nervously.

"I don't think so," he said, taking another step toward her. "You damned little goody-two-shoes, what do you really want from me? Are you going to turn me in?''

She tried to deny it, but her voice was frozen in her throat.

''You're going to betray your own father?''

This said as if it were the worst of crimes. Much worse than poisoning water, killing an EPA man, plotting to poison her boss.

He was moving rapidly toward her. She backed away, wary of the edge of the cliff. They circled gingerly.

''You're not my daughter,'' he said in a harsh voice.

Which she knew meant he had no code at all that he had to honor anymore.

''You're being crazy,'' she told him.

He lunged at her, and she sidestepped, and then turned and ran. She was in far better shape than he, but she was not driven by his desperation. She could hear his footsteps falling heavily on the ground behind her. She could hear the harsh, labored rasp of his breathing.

She thought she had succeeded in putting some distance between them when he tackled her around her knees and brought them both crashing to the ground.

She tried to break free of his hold, but couldn't. He settled heavily on her stomach, right on top of the recorder, pinning her hands on either side of her head.

''What the hell am I sitting on? You're wired?'' He looked stunned, momentarily hurt and afraid, and then furious.

She closed her eyes against the fury in his face. He had become the monster in her dreams.

Suddenly they were illuminated in a strong beam of light. In the distance she could hear sirens.

Her father flipped behind her, pulled her to sitting, wrapped his beefy arm around her neck and dragged her back toward the cliff. Something sleek and hard and cold touched her temple.

She knew, without being able to see, that it was a gun.

"You come a step closer, and I'll kill her," he said. "Turn off the light. *Now.*"

The light winked off.

"Who are they?" he asked her, tightening his grip around her neck. He reached under her sweater, ripped free the tape recorder and smashed it on the ground. "Who are they?" he asked again.

"Some friends of mine."

He gave the recorder a little kick. "Yeah. Got access to some pretty good technology. Who are they? Cops or FBI?"

She said nothing.

"Okay, doll, listen up. I might have just found a way to get me a couple of million anyway. You just became my hostage."

"Why do you want money so badly? Why?"

"Do you live in the real world? Money is everything. It's power and it's privilege. Without it a man is nothing.

"I've given my whole life to Springer. Do you think I ever got invited on the executive holidays, to the executive dinners? Nope, I was just the guy who could be counted on to do the dirty work. They thought I'd work for a pat on the head forever.''

''They made you vice president,'' she said, trying to calm him, trying to make him rational.

''At two-thirds of the salary Corbett made. That actually made me laugh. I was glad I was going to screw them out of a couple of mil. Glad.''

''Daddy, doesn't love count for anything?''

''Don't make me puke.'' He raised his voice. ''Listen to me. I want five million and a helicopter. I want it within the hour. And if I don't get it, your little snitch is going to die.''

''You won't kill me,'' she said loudly.

''I'm backed up against a wall here, Holly. I'll do whatever I have to do.''

She heard the sound of voices over by the road. Male voices. She recognized Blake's. And knew, suddenly, he was coming for her.

Rory and Rafe would try to stop him, might even try to physically restrain him. But they would not succeed.

Then absolute silence reigned. She could feel her father's fear in the slick sweat on his arm where it wrapped around her neck. Out of her peripheral vision, she saw a shadow move. Lamb saw it, too. The metal left her temple, and the sound of a shot exploded the night.

''No,'' she shrieked, and with the superhuman strength born of absolute desperation, she shoved her whole weight back against him. She felt him rock.

She thought she had lost the gamble, when Blake came tearing out of the darkness. Todd took aim, but

Blake was on top of him before the gun went off. It catapulted out of his hand and into the darkness. She heard it clatter down the cliff.

Blake and Todd struggled, so close to the edge of the cliff.

Other men were running toward them now, out of the darkness.

Blake lifted his arm, formed a fist and swung. He hit Todd, and then he hit him again, his face a mask of fury.

They had to pull Blake off of Todd.

They finally succeeded, and he stood there, his chest heaving in and out, his hands loose at his sides.

She got unsteadily to her feet, swayed.

Blake was at her side in a split second, scooped her up in his arms, elbowed through the men who were everywhere.

"Look, renegade," Rory said materializing beside them, "you could have got her killed."

"The way I see it, so could you have," Blake said calmly.

"You jeopardized this whole operation."

"You're lucky my hands are full or I'd give you a fat lip. Negotiate with the bastard! Wear him down. What kind of plan was that?"

"The tried and true kind."

"I'll tell you a kind that's even truer. My heart told me my woman wasn't spending one more second being terrorized by that man. You got it?"

Rory blinked first.

Rafe appeared, shaking his head, and clapped Rory on the shoulder. "Don't think you're going to change him. Better men have tried. Blake, take your woman home.''

"Just a second. We need to debrief. We need—''

"He's right," Rafe told Rory softly. ''There are times to throw the rule book away. Let them go. What she needs right now you can't give her.''

"But—''

"I just have one question for you, Sinclair. What if it had been Peggy?" Blake asked.

Rory was silent, then he looked at his shoe. Then he said, ''Aw, get out of here. I'll drop by and see you in the morning.''

"Late in the morning," Blake said in a way that made shivers run up and down Holly's spine despite how weak she felt, exhausted and emotional.

Rafe handed him the keys to the van.

In what felt like seconds they were at her house. He picked her up and somehow managing to open the door, went through the house and laid her on the bed, kissing her tenderly.

In a moment she heard the bath water running. He came back to the bed and began to take her clothes off.

It was different this time, far different. There was nothing sexual about what he was doing. He wrapped her in a big towel and carried her to the tub. It was full of bubbles, and rimmed by candles. He switched off the lights and helped her into the tub.

She closed her eyes. She tried to feel something, but she didn't. She felt wooden and dead.

He undressed and slipped into the tub behind her. "You can cry now," he said. "It's okay to cry."

She leaned back against his chest, felt his hands encircle her. She closed her eyes, and she began to weep.

For the longest time he said nothing.

And then he said, "You told your father you loved me."

"Ummm."

"Why didn't you tell me?"

"How could I?" she asked. "I felt unworthy. I felt ashamed...of my father. That I didn't figure things out sooner. All these weeks, taking credit for getting the water turned off. He practically told me, and I was too stupid—"

"Stop it."

She had never heard him use that tone of voice with her before. On one of the kids who had done something particularly bad, yes, but never on her. Not even over the incident with Tomas and the knife.

"I won't listen to you talk about yourself like that."

"Blake, this can't work. How can it work? My father—"

"You never seemed to hold it against me that my father took a loaded gun, aimed it at Joe Colton and pulled the trigger."

"It's not like you did it."

"Exactly."

"This is different."

"Okay, tell me how."

But she couldn't. She was too tired.

"You know what I think?" he said softly, "I think it's an amazing piece of kismet that you and I both have less than perfect fathers. I'm going to take it, not as a sign that we're meant to be apart, but a sign that we're meant to be together.

"Forever," he added softly.

"Forever?" she whispered.

"I want you to marry me, Holly Lamb. As soon as that's humanly possible."

She swung around so that she could see his face. He traced the line of her cheek tenderly. She drew his wet finger to her mouth and kissed it.

"You want me to marry you?" she repeated, not sure she could have possibly heard right.

"Yup, you."

"You could have any woman you wanted."

"That's good to know, because I've picked the one I want."

"I mean someone more beautiful than me."

"Doesn't exist."

"Someone more sophisticated."

"Uck."

"Me?" she whispered. "You want me to marry you?"

"Yeah. And soon. As soon as I can get a license and a preacher."

"I have to get through the trial. And my mother will go crazy over this."

"Why? How many husbands has she had since then?"

"Every one of them seemed to be about her failure with him. Trying to prove something to him. Plus, she's very big on what people think. She'll be devastated by this."

"Those sound like good reasons to get married. You need me to support you and to protect you."

"You realize you're saying you're going to have a mother-in-law that people need to be protected from." She actually felt a certain lightness beginning to grow in her, despite everything. It felt like a miracle.

"You're worth it."

"Let's go to bed," she whispered.

"All right. But no hanky-panky tonight."

She could have wept when he said that. Because she knew he was being sensitive to her deepest need.

Just to be held. Loved.

With no ulterior motive, no secret agenda.

"Blake," she whispered, as he slid in the bed beside her and tucked the blankets securely around her. "You know I've loved you forever, don't you?"

"Yes, I know that."

"And," she said sleepily, "that I plan to love you for at least that long?"

"Lucky me."

"And you know why I didn't tell you about what I dreamed, don't you?"

"No, I haven't figured that one out."

"It wasn't because I didn't love you. It was because I loved you too much."

"Okay. I'll accept that as an excuse this once. Don't try and use it again."

"All right, boss."

"Better make that partner, I think."

And then, in the warmth of his arms she slept. The

dream came that night—the same red-skinned monster coming toward her, his rage murderous.

Only, in the dream this time a knight galloped in
on a white horse and slayed the monster and all he
stood for: conditional love, trying to win approval that
never came, trying to be something she could never
be.

And when the knight who had slain the dragon rode
up to her, stopped, lifted his visor and bowed to her,
she smiled.

Blake.

Her knight in shining armor. She snuggled deeper
into the arms that held her.

Forever.

Epilogue

The ivory satin rustled around Holly. She smoothed the dress with her fingertips, smiled. The last few weeks seemed to have passed in a dream, but suddenly it all seemed real.

"Are you nervous?" Jenn squeaked in her ear.

"No," Holly said and it was true. How could she be nervous about something that was so right?

"I am," Jenn said. "Look at all the people! What if I trip and fall flat on my face in front of that crowd? in front of Stephen?"

Holly smiled at her friend. Jenn looked more beautiful than ever. She was madly in love with Stephen Darce, and he with her. Holly suspected there would be another wedding before long.

"I think all of Prosperino is here," Jenn wailed. "There goes the mayor."

Holly peeked out the door. It was true. There was quite a crowd gathered at Hacienda de Alegria this beautiful day.

The sun was shining and flowers bloomed in radiant abundance. The lawns had been manicured, the shrubs trimmed, the fences painted. At least three hundred white chairs formed a half moon around the beautiful pagoda Joe Colton had ordered built just for today.

The thought of Joe deepened the feeling of well-being inside of Holly. He had come to her as soon as Blake had told him of their engagement and their plans to wed quickly.

"Holly," Joe had said, "it would be the greatest honor of my life if you'd allow me to escort you down the aisle, give you away."

She had been too astounded to speak, and Joe had continued.

"Blake is my son, the son of my soul, if not my flesh. And now you will be Meredith's and my daughter, and we couldn't be more tickled."

What Joe Colton had said to her was that he would take the place of the father who could not be there. Todd Lamb was in jail. What Joe Colton had really said was that he, the most respected man in this community, would stand beside her, proudly, completely divorcing her from the crimes of her father.

The father who had never been there.

Holly looked again at the crowd, moving now in colorful groups that dotted the sloping lawns to take their places in the chairs.

Finally, she saw her mother. She had expected that

Rose must be wearing an outlandish outfit that would surely attract more attention than the bride's.

But her mother was in a very mature gray silk suit, and a lovely matching hat.

"You're right," Blake had said thoughtfully. "Let's tell her to go ahead."

And so Rose had gone ahead, her lessons culminating with the wedding.

Holly's mother caught her eye and waved. She mouthed some words.

Beautiful. Her mother thought she was beautiful.

Holly's gaze moved on and found Rafe and Libby.

And then Rory and Peggy.

And then Michael and Suzanne.

Nature knew about balances, too. Nature or fate or God. Whatever you preferred to call that power that was greater than all things.

Some heavenly force had looked down on the horror of that water being poisoned, children becoming ill, the ranch being closed, and had decided some balance was required.

And so love sprang up all around that tragedy.

Love and evil arm-wrestled. And love won.

The children were all back in residence at the Hopechest now, the contamination completely cleared from the water, all the DMBE accounted for and disposed of, the ranch was like a ghost town that had been given a second chance at life. It bustled with activity and energy and laughter.

Holly's feeling of belonging to that ranch and the children on it, filled her to overflowing. It seemed to her it was the most wondrous of miracles that she was going to spend her life on the Hopechest, side by side with the man that she loved.

The music started, and Joe appeared at her side. Jenn gathered her basket of flowers and the train of Holly's dress.

Somehow Rory and Rafe had found Blake and he was standing at the pagoda now, flanked by them, his eyes fastened on the house, waiting for her.

Dimly, she registered the music wasn't "The Wedding March."

Jamie Lynn Barker came forward. And then, in white shirts and blue jeans, the children of the Hopechest Ranch came in solemn lines down the aisles of chairs, and formed neat lines behind Jamie, smallest to tallest. Holly saw Tomas and Lucille and so many of the other children who had passed through her office, sat on her couch, cuddled her teddy bears.

"Meredith's been rehearsing them all week," Joe said proudly. "It's a surprise for you. She heard it was your favorite song."

Jamie's voice soared out alone.

When all else has failed me,
When I'm weary and torn,
Love whispers to me,
And my spirit is reborn.

The children began to hum behind her, and her voice soared even higher, strong and vital.

Oh, I've walked alone
All the days of my life,

But love promises me
An end to heartache and strife.

The voices of the children joined her now, voices full of innocence and wonder. Their voices were full of hope and dreams and promises. They were strong voices, for all that they were childish. Voices that had survived the storm and came out the other side still believing in goodness.

Joe stepped forward, and they walked down the aisle to the joyous song of the children. Holly struggled not to cry as she followed his lead, allowed herself to feel his strength and his steadiness. Strength and steadiness that would always be available to her now.

Because today she was not just marrying Blake. She was becoming a part of something larger than herself.

A family. Today all her dreams were coming true.

Like the sailor who comes home from the sea,
The warrior home from the dying;
Bring your broken wings to me.
Love mends those hearts that are crying.

Blake saw that she was coming now, floating down the aisle, a vision in that ivory gown that spilled over the hands of her bridesmaid and swept the grass.

He could not take her eyes off her.

She was radiant.

More radiant than the sun.

The music seemed to lift her up on its wings, and

he could feel the pure emotion of those childrens' voices clawing at his own throat.

She looked absolutely beautiful. But he alone, of all the people here, knew the best thing of all. She would still be the most beautiful woman in the world even if she put her glasses back on, and her hair back up, and those suits back on.

Well, maybe he had to draw the line at the suits.

But this was the secret he knew: She was more beautiful on the inside than she could ever be on the outside.

And she had said yes to him. She was going to join him in this wonderful new adventure.

"Who gives this woman?"

Joe said firmly, "I do."

And she walked the final few steps alone. She took his hand, and the trembling within him quieted as they walked up the stairs of the pagoda together.

"Dearly beloved," the minister said, "we are gathered here in celebration of the love between a man and a woman."

Who would have thought the events of the last few months would end like this? In celebration of love?

He thought of that moment, weeks ago now, when he had pondered the nature of miracles. He had only asked for one more: That the children be returned to the ranch.

But he had heard it said that God knew so much better than an ordinary mortal what that man needed.

And God had given him the miracle he had never dared ask for. Not even when he was a little boy.

God had given him someone to love him.

Blake took her hand and lifted it to his mouth, kissed it gently, met her eyes. Her eyes shone with tears, and love and laughter.

And held his future in their depths.

He knew the dream that had been planned for him was better than anything he could have ever dreamed for himself.

There were no words big enough to express that, but the two that came from his lips seemed like they would suffice, an affirmation of love and of life, an acceptance of the gift of love, a promise to do his best to be worthy of the immense and amazing gift the universe had given him.

"I do," Blake Fallon said firmly. "I do."

* * * * *

world's most
Eligible Bachelors

RICH, GORGEOUS, SEXY AND SINGLE!

Millionaire To Marry
by
RACHEL LEE

He was rugged, rich and sexy as sin...
Yet Jeff Cumberland had managed to avoid every
marriage-minded female in Conard County.
It seemed that no one could get close to the elusive
rancher. Until a mysterious woman breezed
into town in need of his protection.

Available from 18th April 2003

Even the wealthiest, sexiest, most powerful men
fall hard... when they fall in love.

**SILHOUETTE®
SPECIAL EDITION™**

*proudly presents seven more fantastic stories
from*

Lindsay McKenna's

exciting series

MORGAN'S MERCENARIES

*Meet Morgan's newest team:
courageous men and women destined for
greatness—fated to fall in love!*